WAR OF THE CARDS

COLLEEN OAKES

First published in the US by HarperTeen in 2017
HarperTeen is a division of HarperCollins*Publishers*
Published in Great Britain by HarperCollins *Children's Books* in 2018
HarperCollins *Children's Books* is a division of HarperCollins*Publishers* Ltd,
HarperCollins Publishers
1 London Bridge Street
London SE1 9GF

The HarperCollins website address is:
www.harpercollins.co.uk

1

ISBN 978–0–00–817545–0

Printed and bound by CPI Group (UK) Ltd, Croydon CR0 4YY

To all the girls with dark hearts and those who dare to love them

"I can't explain myself, I'm afraid, sir.

Because I'm not myself, you see."

— Alice's Adventures in Wonderland *by Lewis Carroll*

One

Dinah chased a white rabbit, just beyond her reach. It turned and veered under rosebushes and vertically stacked tables piled with teacups. She turned a corner. It was gone. She turned again. A wave crashed over her, only instead of being wet, it was made of fire, a fire that thundered in her heart. The rabbit was there again, taunting her. As she watched, it swung its pocket watch back and forth, hypnotizing her. The rabbit's ears began to shrink down into its head before her. Its eyes were swallowed by its changing face, which was becoming elongated and sharp. Feathers blossomed out of its back as it turned into a white peacock. It opened its mouth to speak. Its voice was high and sweet, the disembodied voice of Faina Baker. "Keep your temper, Queen of Hearts. . . ."

"We're here, Your Majesty." The gentle voice of her Yurkei guard jerked her out of sleep. Dinah's eyes blinked open as Morte came to an uneasy stop.

It was unbelievable to her that she had fallen asleep while riding this temperamental animal, but there was something so lulling about Morte's gait. That, and she was exhausted. They had been marching toward Wonderland Palace for many days, and sleep had not been a frequent visitor to Dinah's bed. All her dreams of late were filled with nightmarish images. In the dawn hours just before she woke, her mind was battered with images of Wardley, the love of her life, who had fractured her heart into a thousand jagged pieces. Wardley, naked and glistening with sweat. Wardley, kissing her as red rose petals fell around them. Wardley, an old withered man, dying in her arms, his heart a hardened black shell that beat outside his body.

It wasn't just him visiting her sleep. There was the dead

farmer that she had found as she outran the Cards in the Twisted Wood, an arrow quivering in his back. There was the Heart Cards she had killed on her way out of Charles's room, their blood chasing her down an endless palace hallway.

These nightmares made for poor sleep, and Dinah awoke each morning with a pounding head and a heavy, jaded heart. She would sit up and slowly pull on her clothing, reminding herself why she was here: because she was the rightful Queen of Wonderland and she had come to conquer her kingdom. Most mornings, the thought was enough to motivate her. Other times, she lay in bed wishing that she was anywhere but here, in a damp tent that smelled of the Spades.

After pulling on her tunic, cloaks, and boots, Dinah would sit on the edge of her bed and clutch at her chest, hoping to smother the black fury inside her. The fury whispered to her that she would never be loved and made her mouth water at the mention of blood.

She would slowly push the rage back inside and struggle to control it. Then she would put on her crown, emerge from her tent, say good morning to her Yurkei bodyguards, greet her advisers—Sir Gorrann, Cheshire, Starey Belft, and Bah-kan—and climb on her devil steed. Her army would continue making their way north.

Each calculated, queenly step was exhausting. Her waking hours were filled with both longing and hatred for Wardley. She carried the weight of her love for him on her shoulders and in her chest. As they had marched north from the Darklands, he rode behind her, his eyes never leaving her back for long. Everywhere she turned, he was there, and each time their eyes met, Dinah was flooded with fresh pain.

They hadn't spoken since that afternoon beside the waterfall, when he had broken her heart into pieces. But it wasn't for Wardley's lack of trying. Every afternoon, he greeted Dinah with a tray of lunch and awkwardly attempted to explain himself to her. She brushed him off without words, leaving him in the tent with the tray of bread in his hands. He was desperate for her forgiveness, and she would not give it, not now when the sight of him made her physically sick. Dinah knew that he wished for her to know he still cared for her. What he couldn't understand was that for Dinah, it was torturous to see him. Two nights ago, when she awoke to him sitting on the edge of her bed and staring at her, Dinah finally forced her mouth to form the words.

"Wardley." Her voice was barely a pleading whisper, choked with a restrained sob. "Please, leave me alone. I can't bear to be near you right now."

Wardley reached for her hand, but Dinah turned away and buried herself under a Yurkei feather blanket.

"If you care for me, you will leave."

Finally, when it became apparent that she would not speak with him, Wardley sighed and stood. "Please don't cut me off from you."

"Go!" she snapped.

"Fine. I'll do as you ask now. But I will not leave your side once the battle begins, so don't ask me. I don't care what you command. Do you understand?"

Dinah finally gave a slight nod, praying that he would leave before her tears overtook her. She heard the tent flap open, and when she turned around he had vanished into the early morning darkness, leaving her alone with a shattered heart.

Days had passed since then, and the pain was as fresh as an open wound.

"It's good to take a break, Your Majesty," muttered Ki-ershan, one of her two Yurkei bodyguards.

Dinah blinked in the sunlight. Morte stamped impatiently. She took a minute to shake herself awake and glanced behind her. The sight was staggering. Thousands of men were spread across the plains, like an ominous shadow that passed over the land. A hundred yards behind her, her advisers rode in an unregimented clump. Behind them, a line of two thousand Yurkei warriors on their sleek steeds moved smoothly as if they were of one mind. From up here, she thought, you would never know that they were a mostly peaceful and pleasant people. From here, they looked like a dark blot of death. Dinah swallowed hard.

As they would be, for those who fought for the king.

Almost half a mile behind the Yurkei marched the weary Spades and rogue Cards, a large horde of cantankerous and brutal men clothed in black that inched slowly across the grass-blown plain. They were all fighting for Dinah, but they fought for their own reasons: the Spades because of their unequal status within the Cards, the Yurkei because of hundreds of years of violent grievances with Wonderland Palace. A vastly larger group of Yurkei soldiers led by their chief, Mundoo, marched their way to Wonderland Palace from the north. Dinah and her motley bunch were to meet them there on the day of battle.

They would crush the larger Card army from both sides—Mundoo attacking from the north side of Wonderland Palace, and Dinah's much smaller troop coming in from the south—with the idea that two armies would be a bigger psychological as well as a strategic threat.

She hoped it would work.

It was all Cheshire's planning.

Dinah rode Morte out front, alone. She didn't have much use for company lately. Silently, she watched as Wardley raised his arm and the brigade came to a sudden halt. The sound of the men's obvious relief reached Dinah's ears. *I must remember that no matter how tired I am, I am not as weary as my men.* Wardley brought Corning up beside her, with Bah-kan following grumpily at his heels.

"Why did we stop?" Bah-kan bellowed. "We are almost

to the villages of Wonderland proper."

Dinah cleared her throat and looked away from Wardley. The sight of his face made her heart twist so painfully that she almost lost her breath. "Please communicate to the army that we are camping here for the night."

Wardley's eyes lingered pitifully on her face before he spurred Corning off to aid the Spades with setting up camp.

Bah-kan growled in Dinah's direction. "The Yurkei won't be happy about this."

"Thank you for telling me," replied Dinah coldly. "I will keep that in mind."

He was right, of course. The Yurkei were a thousand times more physically fit than the Spades, but more important, they rode horses that never seemed to tire. The Yurkei's wild herds were miraculous beasts, and the Spades appeared quite taken with them. The warriors from Hu-Yuhar had mistakenly assumed they would be marching straight to Wonderland with very little time to stop and camp. The vast majority of the Spades were walking, and so they rightly required more breaks. This had led to an ever-growing discontent that only inflamed the two groups' hatred for each other. In addition to this, the long march to Wonderland Palace had taken a deep physical toll on the men. While they had expected the march to take upward of two weeks, Dinah was surprised at just how difficult it was to move her small army.

Getting the Yurkei south had been easy compared to this. Returning the Spades back to where they'd just come from was an endless litany of negotiations, disappointment, and hunger. Most of them were not completely at ease with a woman leading them and directed their questions and complaints to Starey Belft, Cheshire, or Wardley.

While she at times quietly doubted her own ability to lead, she didn't want her men doing it. Because of this, Dinah begrudgingly made it a point to interact with the men as much as possible. She joined them for dinner, watched their sparring bouts, and attempted to engage them in casual conversation. She made sure to personally thank each one for his loyalty. Yet despite all this effort, they still looked to Cheshire for answers. Around Dinah they acted shy but respectful. There was a lot of staring.

Dinah apparently wasn't the only one being stared at.

Yur-Jee, her fierce Yurkei guard, was staring with seething hatred at a Spade soldier who was attempting to feed one of the Yurkei steeds a piece of bread. Yur-Jee's hand clutched his bow as he gestured frantically to the Spade.

"Lu-yusa! Ilu-fre!" He stumbled for broken Wonderlander, finally finding the word. "No!"

The Spade, a husky man with a giant black beard and red-rimmed eyes, stepped back.

"What the hell is he going on about now?" he grumbled.

Yur-Jee was climbing off his horse, tight, lean muscles tensing as his feet hit the ground. The Spade reached for his ax.

"Stop! Ja-Hohy!"

Both men wisely paused at the voice of their future queen. Dinah carefully dismounted Morte, sliding down half his body as her calloused hands clutched his red leather rein.

"Idiots!" she quietly whispered to herself as she closed the space between them. When she reached the men, she calmly took the bread out of the Spade's hand and tossed it on the ground before meeting the Spade's eyes. She heard a familiar nicker behind her from Cyndy, Sir Gorrann's mare. She was reassured by his quiet presence.

Altercations like this seemed to happen every other hour, and she was learning to deal with them one by one. Ruling, it turned out, was terribly tedious and made up of a dozen small decisions every day that seemed to always upset someone. She smiled kindly at the Spade, who stared at her unnervingly.

"The Yurkei only let their horses eat wild grasses, did you know that? This special diet is what we believe gives them their endurance."

The Spade snorted. "Fancy diet, yeh say? For their horses? That's a load of shit if I've ever heard it."

He spit on the ground at Dinah's feet. Behind her, Sir Gorrann cleared his throat to reprimand the man, but Dinah raised her hand, silencing him. She leveled the soldier with a glare.

"Should you disrespect me again, you'll find yourself in shackles at the end of the line, trying your best to keep up with their steeds. If you choose differently—say, to make your way back to your post and take it upon yourself to educate others that they are not to feed the Yurkei steeds—then you may end this journey without raw wrists and bleeding feet." She tilted her head, ignoring the urge to strike this man repeatedly.

The man dropped his eyes and bent to his knee. Dinah smiled. "It's just, we're tired, miss. The savage—" Dinah's hand went to her sword at the word, but the man backed up. "Sorry. It's just that the Yurkei all have horses, and we have none. I lost one toe on the march already, and I thought if I gave one some food, then maybe . . ."

"It would let you ride it? That the Yurkei warrior would walk?"

Dinah knew this would never happen—the Yurkei were deeply connected to their steeds—and yet she understood the inequality of being forced to walk all day most days when others rode. It wasn't just about the horses; this was a bitterness that predated her reign by several decades.

Dinah had imagined herself leading an army of brave men with herself at the helm, arriving in glory and with great fanfare. Instead, she spent most of her time trying to make peace between the two factions that fought for her. She motioned for Yur-Jee to return to his horse and lead on. He nodded, and briefly Dinah recognized the obedience she'd fought so hard to gain. Her black eyes simmering, she bent over the Spade. Her newly short black hair brushed her chin.

"I hear your cries, but disrespecting the Yurkei will get you nowhere. I will offer you this: take care of the Yurkei steeds on the march. When we camp for the night, brush them, feed them—wild grasses only—and make sure they are checked for injuries. If you do this and do it well, once I am queen I will remove you from the Spades and put you in charge of incorporating the Yurkei's understanding of animal husbandry into our new, united kingdom. We have much to learn from them."

The Spade was sputtering now, tears forming in his eyes. What she had offered was unthinkable for a man who had never been allowed property, rights, or titles in any way.

"Yes, my queen." He began kissing her hand repeatedly, his scratchy beard tickling her wrist.

"I'm not queen yet," Dinah stated. "But let's change that, shall we?"

The Spade walked away, and for a moment Dinah was

proud of how she had comported herself.

With Cheshire's help, Dinah was learning that it was far better to put offenders to use rather than impose harsh punishments. She would be foolish to do so, for it would mean the loss of these skilled fighters. This same strategy shaped her entire plan for the battle. The war council met nightly in a heavily guarded tent, always coming to the same impasse: the men would argue for lots of casualties, and yet Dinah repeated herself, again and again, "I will not hurt my people if I don't have to." Once Cheshire had reluctantly agreed, the plan moved forward.

At their most recent council meeting, Bah-kan had pushed himself up dangerously close to Dinah, his huge face bursting with veins. "How will we hold back the Cards if we cannot kill them? How are we to win when we must keep men alive? This is nonsense! You are sending us to our graves."

Dinah's face remained calm in the presence of his boiling anger, though she longed to strike him. "The Cards who fight for the King of Hearts will become my men once the war is over. I do not wish to inherit an empty palace with only ghosts to haunt its walls. We *must* make prisoners of as many as we can. We will spill blood in the first wave; that can't be helped. May the gods have mercy on those men who face our swords first. But Bah-Kan, we also must be merciful. To win this battle—and the battle for the hearts and minds of the people—we must get to the king as quickly as possible. That is our priority."

"The king will fight," protested Starey Belft. "But he will don his armor and ride out with the mounted Heart Cards on the north side, to face Mundoo's army. He is a fierce warrior but tires easily. As soon as the battle turns, he will retreat back inside the keep to wait for you there, sharpening his Heartsword."

Dinah felt a twinge of fear mixed with something alarmingly seductive deep inside her. "By that time, our army should be pressing against the gates, or, by the grace of the gods, inside the gates."

"We cannot assume that we will be inside." Cheshire spoke quietly, as always, his long hands folded underneath his chin. "The majority of the king's Cards will be on the north side to counter Mundoo's army, but he will no doubt spare a few thousand for our army on the south end of the palace. We will have to cut our way to the gates, open them, get inside, make it through the palace grounds, and open up the gates on the north side so that Mundoo's forces can enter. But if we cannot get inside quickly, the Cards will make a graveyard of our forces. We do not have the men or resources to lay a siege. We must win the first push, or else we will lose."

There was a silence in the tent as each man and one queen weighed their fates.

Wardley broke the silence. "The king will unleash all his power. He'll use innocent people in unthinkable ways. And then there is the matter of the Fergal archers. . . ." He rubbed his lips, and for a second Dinah tasted them against her own. "The battle will descend into chaos quickly, where both sides will be taking heavy losses. Dinah's right—we *must* overtake the king as quickly as possible. That is our purpose. Once that happens, Dinah can seize power quickly and the fighting will stop. When she is the sole ruler of Wonderland, the people will bend their knees and submit to her authority. They will have no choice. Remember, most of them *fear* the king. They've lost loved ones to his paranoia and rage. Most of these men are bakers, spoiled members of the court, farmers, fishmongers. . . ."

"Or highly trained Heart Cards," countered Dinah.

"Yes." Bah-kan ran his fingers over his blade as if strumming an instrument. "Whoever they are, we will give them no choice. They will bow to the Queen of Hearts or they will die. Then we will execute the highest-ranking Cards to remind them of her power."

Wardley flicked his hair out of his face, annoyed, and though Dinah's heart gave a pang of pain, her face remained motionless. She turned to Bah-kan.

"No, we will not. All who declare their loyalty to me will be cleared of any charges and allowed to continue with their lives. It is the quickest way to get Wonderland back to a functioning kingdom. We cannot risk a divided city when winter is near. We'll need every baker, fisherman, and Card." Dinah raised her chin and the men around her nodded their consent. "When I am crowned queen, we will grant mercy to those who want it. Is this understood?"

"And to those who kill our men? Our warriors? Or

what of those high-ranking court members who aided the king?" Bah-kan was stalking around the room, scowling at everyone who looked in his direction. "I've seen what Cards do to the Yurkei they capture. It is unforgivable. They have taken our lands, raped our women. . . ."

"Spoken by a man who once called himself the greatest Card to ever live?" snapped Starey Belft. He turned to the group. "Do you mean that you've taken their lands and raped their women? Before you turned? Before you became one of *them*?" His voice rose. "How dare you speak against them when you were once a Card yourself?"

Bah-kan lunged for Belft but was blocked by Wardley, who leaped in between them. All parties fell to the ground in a fury of fists and shouts. Cheshire raised his eyebrow at Dinah from across the room. Her head throbbed as they tumbled at her feet. Fury rose into her chest; she had had enough.

"Sit down!" she thundered, rising to her feet. "Enough, all of you!" The three men stared at her with shock. "I am your queen and you will listen to my command. I order you to stop acting like spoiled children with your imagined hurts and prejudices. You are no better than the men out there in the tents, looking for any excuse to beat on each other. We are their leaders, and we must project to our men that we are *one army*. If you cannot control your emotions, how am I to believe that you can lead these men and warriors into battle?"

She whirled, unleashing her ferocity on the men seated around her.

"Bah-kan, control your temper, or this council will know your absence. Starey Belft, you may not insult Bah-kan or any Yurkci again, not in or outside of my presence. He has made his choice, and he has been an essential ally in our fight. Now, we will continue with our discussion in a civilized and dignified manner."

The men sat like obedient children, and it occurred to Dinah that what all these warriors might need was a strong mother with a whipping spoon. She rubbed her forehead. "You have disappointed me tonight. You are dismissed."

In silence, they filed out of the tent.

That night, as Dinah undressed for bed, she was filled with a surge of pride. *Without a trace of fear, I just belittled the greatest collection of warriors I've ever seen. Perhaps there is hope that I can be the queen that Wonderland deserves.* This thought followed her pleasantly into sleep, but her subconscious proved to be the enemy of rest.

In her dreams, the King of Hearts stood beside her, his massive red cape snapping around them like a cold wind as they stood on a pile of Yurkei corpses. He pointed his finger at her. "I'm waiting for you."

Dinah cried out in her sleep, but there was no one around to hear her.

Two

The long march north toward Wonderland Palace continued. The landscape gradually changed from the Darklands' marshy bogs into sweeping green expanses marked occasionally by gray crags of rocks. The rocks were covered with strange etchings that only the Yurkei seemed to understand.

Today had been one of those rare days where Dinah didn't have to speak to Wardley at all. Those were the good days, when her heart wasn't bleeding out and her chest wasn't constantly aching with longing.

Without meaning to, Dinah had isolated herself from the rest of her council: Sir Gorrann with his kind words and blunt advice was taxing to her nerves, Starey Belft with his grumpy mutterings made her reach for her sword. Her two Yurkei guards stayed a couple of horse lengths away from her at all times, sensing that she wasn't in the mood for company. The only person that she could occasionally tolerate was Cheshire. He hid nothing from her and didn't patronize. His emotionless words of war, locations, statistics, and schemes were like warm milk down her throat.

At the front of her line she sat numbly on Morte, feeling like a queen only in that she was wearing her small ruby crown. Disturbing fantasies of revenge and violence were a strange source of relief that she could indulge fully during the long hours of silent marching.

Sometimes, she imagined that Wardley would appear in the door of her tent. With his curly brown hair plastered across his forehead, his large hands would trace her cheeks. His trembling voice would confess that something had changed and that all he had ever needed was her. He would kiss her lips softly before lifting her up to meet him, and then both would be wrapped up in an ecstasy of love and passion. It didn't happen. Deep inside her, where the core of anger was always churning now, she knew it would never be. Even if they were destructive, these images kept her awake and kept her face still and strong in front of her men. Dinah knew that no matter how she was feeling inside, she couldn't project anything less than a statuesque strength. If she faltered, her rule would end before it began.

As the sun simmered high in the sky that afternoon, Dinah felt as though they would never be at the palace, that they would just march until they walked into the sea. With the hot sun bearing down on them, it would have been a welcome break.

She heard thundering hooves as Starey Belft rode up behind her. She closed her eyes. *Please be good news*, she thought. His grave face threw water on that theory.

"Another one?"

Starey nodded. "Yes, Your Majesty. A young one, marching near the back. His name was Kingsley." The commander of the Spades paused. "He was a good lad. Had a knack for the lyre and a dirty joke."

Oh gods, a young one. Dinah nodded. "Thank you for telling me."

Starey placed his horse in front of Morte, who snorted angrily. "That's the second one in two days. We need a break. We need to burn our men and tend to our bleeding feet."

Dinah's eyes narrowed. "I am not unaware of your sufferings. But we must meet Mundoo at the right time or this battle will be lost."

Starey wheeled around. "If you keep marching at this pace, you won't have an army to meet him."

Dinah dismissed him with a wave. "I'll take it under consideration."

Starey turned his horse and muttered something under his breath as he moved past her. Anger ignited underneath her skin, and the black fury that was eating her from within moved her muscles without her permission. Dinah saw a flash of red, and suddenly she was swinging her leg up and around Morte's neck, her hand reaching out to grab ahold of Starey Belft's reins. With a wild leap, she crossed the gap between their two steeds and found herself seated behind the

Spade commander, with one arm wrapped around his waist and the other holding a dagger. The sharp blade pressed into his neck.

"Do you want to say that again?" she whispered. "Say it so everyone can hear."

Starey looked around with bewilderment. Dinah's two Yurkei guards halted, their eyes wide with confusion.

Dinah pressed the blade harder. "Say it."

Starey's heart was hammering—Dinah could feel it through the back of his body. Her own heart loved the sound the fear made.

"I said . . ." He cleared his throat. "I said you're just like your father, building a kingdom by the blood of our backs."

"That's what I thought you said." She leaned forward, her black hair brushing his chin. "I march for you, do you know that? I march for the Spades, and for you, Starey Belft. Someday when I am queen, there will be no mutterings about me or my father."

Her eyes met Cheshire's, who was watching the scene with elation. It shook her out of the moment. The red faded from her eyes, and the black fury curled back into its sleeping place inside her. *What the hells was she doing?* Dinah dropped the dagger with surprise.

"Do not question me again," she said weakly as she climbed off his horse.

The Spade commander stared at her for a long moment. Their eyes met and Dinah held his gaze until he looked away. *Yes, that's right*, she thought. *I am your master.*

He coughed. "If we could have a funeral for the lads, that'd be nice. That's all I was saying, Yer Majesty."

"I think that's a lovely idea."

Dinah vaulted back up into the saddle with Morte's help. After a moment, she raised her eyes to the sky, where a heavy rainstorm was blowing their way.

"We will stop marching for now. The men will have a break. Let's set up camp for the night."

"But Dinah, if we are late . . ." Wardley's voice shook her inside out.

"I know the consequences," Dinah snapped.

With a click of her tongue, she plunged away from him,

letting Morte take her and her anger far away from those trying to help.

♥

Later that evening, heavy rain from the storm blustered around them. The few Yurkei warriors who they had sent on ahead appeared as swift-moving black dots on the flat horizon. They declared that they were maybe only three days from the palace gates. *My gods, three days.* Dinah felt the words in the pit of her stomach, the news both invigorating and terrifying.

However, it was very welcome news to the Spades, who were beginning to look less like fearsome warriors and more like wearied travelers. The camps had seemed to be in good spirits, with laughter rising up into the afternoon sky. Dinah smiled when she heard it. Laughter these days was rare and welcome, and the sound of these grizzled men tinkled over the land like a baby's giggle.

That evening, after the storm, the clouds broke wide open, and a flawless sky shimmered with stars. The bodies of the two fallen Spades were being laid down on a pile of wood. Clothed in a white dress and black cloak, Dinah looked over their bodies. She was surprised but not embarrassed by the tears in her eyes. She reached out a trembling hand and touched every whisker on the men's faces before cradling their blackened, cracked heels in her hands.

Remember this, she told herself. *Remember these men, and the physical cost of your reign.* She let a silent tear drip down her face as she bent over them, saying empty prayers to the Wonderland gods. Her hands were placed over their still hearts, hoping to absorb their strength and take on their mission—hoping to make it through the battle they would never see.

Sir Gorrann handed her a spitting torch, and with grim determination Dinah set their bodies aflame. She stood motionless and held back tears, watching the skin of her men pull back as it slowly cooked, veins and muscle turning from living flesh into drifting flakes of ash. A large circle of black-clad Spades stood around her, all reaching forward with one hand, fully present for the last moment with their fallen comrades.

An eerie sound rose up from the other side of the camp,

and Dinah clenched her teeth. It was the wails of the Yurkei.

Cheshire stepped forward and bowed his head, his purple cloak flapping behind him as he came to a stop beside her.

"They cry because they feel that we are imprisoning the souls of the Spades here in Wonderland instead of freeing them in the ground. It's either that or that they believe we are releasing poison ash into the air. Actually, Your Majesty, it's probably both."

Dinah raised an eyebrow but said nothing. Ki-ershan had tried to warn her that the funerals would be a problem, but Dinah knew she had no choice; the men must be burned and the Spades must be appeased.

Her eyes lingered over the burning bodies of the men, and she jumped backward when they met the glowing eyes of Iu-Hora, the Yurkei's doctor and the man they called the Caterpillar. His stare passed through her, seeing every thought, every dark desire. With a wicked smile, he nodded at her before disappearing into the Darklands. Dinah looked away, keeping her eyes on her fallen Spades. The Yurkei continued their loud lament, tossing insults casually across the divide.

"I'm not going to listen to this horseshit!" spat one of the Spades to her right. Dinah could feel the rising tempers of the Spades around her.

Sir Gorrann raised his arms. "Now, if everyone would just calm down. Let's say farewell to our friends and then I'll get yeh a drink. More than one."

Someone started pushing forward, and Dinah found herself shoved toward the towering funeral pyre. Cheshire caught her arm and yanked her backward, saving her from a wide lick of flame. She turned, unnerved by what she saw. The barrier between the camps was lined with Spades and Yurkei facing one another, casting insults and mocking the other side.

As the flames grew higher, a sort of war hysteria was taking over the men. Starey Belft was hollering at the men at the top of his lungs, but his words were ignored. Wardley was galloping Corning up and down the line between the Spades and the Yurkei camp, daring anyone to cross the line. As gallant as he looked, he wasn't imposing enough to stem the years of hatred that were boiling over. Dinah began violently shoving her way to the center. Sir Gorrann was beside her, his sword out, shoving Spades left and right as they tried to pass through a passionate throng that barely noticed them.

As the Yurkei's cries of complaint rose into the sky, the Spades became unhinged, urged on by their exhaustion and grief. A few mugs of ale were lazily thrown at the Yurkei, who dodged them calmly. The Spades began spitting on the ground and cursing, blaming the Yurkei for the death of their friends.

Dread rose in Dinah's heart as she ran forward. She had always known that her army was a simmering pot of decades-old discord and bloodlust. She had foolishly hoped that if she could just get the men to Wonderland proper, their common enemy would unite them.

"Out of the way!" she screamed, shoving aside a Spade who looked at her with disbelief. "Stand down!" She kept yelling it, but her voice was swallowed in the tide.

The Spade next to her drew his mace, and Dinah knew in that moment they would never make it to the line in time. The unrest in the air was so thick that she could almost smell it over the repulsive smell of burned bodies. After that, it all happened so quickly. Axes raised, two Spades burst out of line behind Wardley and Corning and charged toward a circle of chanting warriors. The Yurkei saw them coming and quickly nocked their arrows, aiming their points directly at the Spades' hearts.

Dinah flung her torch to the ground and sprinted after the two Spades, her hands out in front of her. "Stop! Gods, stop! They aren't the enemy!" she screamed, but it might as well have been the wind.

They ran forward naively, for Dinah understood what the Spades did not: that the Yurkei would win any confrontation, and when they did, it would be a massacre. Every Spade on this field would die.

The Yurkei released their arrows, which flew impossibly fast toward the Spades' unprotected hearts. One of the Spades flung an ax into the crowd of the Yurkei. It was all going to end.

As her feet pounded the ground, Dinah heard a strange scraping sound and looked up to see the flame on the funeral pyre being sucked into the sky like a funnel.

Like the breath of an angry god, the Sky Curtain arrived.

A giant crack ricocheted through the sky, so loud that it sent Spade and Yurkei alike to their knees in fear, as if the gods themselves were breaking open the heavens. Dinah fell to the ground, but barely had time to cover her head before there was someone covering her body with his own.

She was five years old when the Sky Curtain had appeared over the Twisted Wood. All of Wonderland Palace had stopped what it was doing to watch. Members of the court and peasants alike had climbed up on their roofs to get a better view of the curtain. The streets had been flooded with people; pickpockets ran rampant. Young Dinah had climbed up on her castle balcony for a better view. She had stepped on the end of her nightgown and would have tumbled to her death if it was not for Harris scooping her up in his arms. After she was duly reprimanded, Harris put her on his wide shoulders so she could better see the curtain fluttering over the mountains. From where Dinah sat, it looked as though a giant had gathered a handful of the stars and yanked downward. Everyone living had only heard of this natural phenomenon in history books. Even as a child, it had taken her breath away. "Harris, what is it?"

"It's a miracle from the Wonderland gods, my queen," he said through his sniffled sobs. "Can't you see?"

Dinah turned her head, her long, braided black hair flopping against her face. "Who is it for? Is it for me? Why does it come? How do I get it? Why is it over the Twisted Wood?"

Harris shrugged. Dinah giggled as her body flopped up and down on his shoulders.

"You have so many impatient questions, Your Majesty! You must wait for the answers to come before rattling off more questions." He sighed. "Some say that it comes when the weather is just right, when the wind from the Western Slope meets with the wet air from the Darklands and the salty sands of the Todren."

"But you don't believe that?"

Harris shook his head. "I believe it's a gift. A gift for someone who needs it. Just look at it. How could it not be seen as anything but a miracle?" They silently watched it from the palace balcony until it disappeared a few minutes later. Both were left stunned by its massive size and awe-inspiring divinity.

Harris slowly lifted Dinah off his shoulders and put her back down in her feathered bed. But she was too riled up to sit still. She bounced toward the door.

"I'm going to tell Father about the Sky Curtain!"

Harris shook his head. "He's busy, Princess. Let's not bother him."

Dinah let her hand linger on the red glass handle. "He's not busy. He doesn't want to see me."

Harris gathered her under his arm. "Let's just keep our gift to ourselves, all right?" His eyes wandered down the hallway. "Unfortunately, I have a feeling your father will not see this as a good thing." Dinah's eyes filled with tears, but she had listened to her wise guardian.

That following winter was the worst winter that Wonderland had ever seen. Thousands of people froze to death in their houses. Gray corpses littered the street and birds fell from their nests with ice-covered chicks hidden under their wings. Crops had frozen on the vine, and hunger was as widespread as the silent panic. Pink snow covered the palace, burying the doors beneath massive drifts that blew from courtyard to courtyard. Just when it seemed the kingdom could survive no longer, warm summer winds blew down from the Western Slope, thawing the snow and ice, and leaving all of Wonderland to dig themselves out.

Harris had been wrong. The Sky Curtain hadn't been a gift.

It was a warning.

♥

Dinah pushed against the body on top of her, recognizing his smell immediately—a smell like cream and leaves and horse.

"Wardley, get off me!"

"No."

She realized in that moment that she would rather die by whatever split the sky than be this close to the man she could never have. It was torture, worse than anything they could ever do to her in the Black Towers. Her voice was muffled as he pushed her head into the dirt. "Get off. It's an order."

He stayed still. Finally she pulled the dagger out of her boot and pressed the tip of it gently against his stomach.

"Get off." She felt his shoulders sag in defeat.

"Dinah . . ."

She crawled out from underneath him and shakily got to her feet. She couldn't see the Yurkei anymore. They were cut off from her, divided by the Sky Curtain.

She gasped. *It couldn't be.* "No." She took a step closer.

Stretching down from the stars, the midnight-blue curtain divided the line between Yurkei and Spade. It was perhaps a mile across and made of the night sky. It had swallowed the Yurkei's arrows and the Spade's ax. It rippled in the wind, like a thick fabric left in front of an open window. Pulled from the sky and cascading down to earth, it brushed the ground in front of Dinah's feet. It gave the slightest tremor as Dinah came near it, as if it recognized her. She could see her reflection in its glossy surface, while at the same time staring deep into its unfathomable and ancient depths. Within its rippling body, stars blinked back at her, so close that she could touch them. A physical piece of the sky brushed the earth. It was a void, the sky and the heavens all at once, and it was draped at her feet, preventing her two armies from destroying each other.

Beside her, Cheshire was getting to his feet, his

always-confident face unmasked with complete disbelief. Starey Belft's mouth was hanging open as she approached him.

"It's not the king!" he yelled out, before turning toward the Spades, who had obviously assumed the same. They dropped their weapons in awe. "It's"—he paused and lowered his voice to an awed whisper—"it's something I believed I would never see again." As Dinah raised her eyes, her sword lowered.

"Sweet gods," she whispered.

The men stayed where they were, rightly terrified of the phenomenon happening in front of them.

Dinah moved forward, fascinated. Somehow, she knew it had come for her.

She stood in front of it now, equally terrified by its godlike presence and seduced by its beauty. Her eyes filled with tears as she wished that Harris could be here, to see the thing that had so touched his heart years ago.

A small thistle by Dinah's feet blew in the curtain's soft wind. Celestial bodies spun and moved inside the shifting cloak, their depths unfathomable and ancient. There was no doubt that all of Wonderland could see it, such was its height. The king, wherever he was, was surely looking out at it. It made Dinah glad. She walked closer, taking in its incredible beauty. All sound around her was sucked out of the air, so that the only thing she heard was the slight snapping of the curtain, like a small flag tossed in a breeze.

Far off, someone was screaming, but it was as if they were underwater. "Dinah! Stop! Don't get too close to it!"

She turned around and saw Cheshire running toward her, his purple cape flapping around him. He held his hand out, waving for her to step back. Sir Gorrann was behind him, hollering swear words at her in two different languages, looking furious, as always. The Spades all stared up at the curtain, their faces contorted with fear and amazement. She smiled. *Silly men.*

Her eyes followed the dirt back to Wardley, who was sitting on the ground next to Corning, his face pale as he stared at her.

"Don't . . . Dinah." He shook his head softly, but Dinah had already turned away.

She dropped her sword and stepped up to the curtain.

Though she couldn't explain it, she knew that she had nothing to fear. Reaching out a steady hand, she dipped her fingers into the curtain. They disappeared for a moment and then they were on the other side, weightless. She turned her hand, feeling everything and nothing. A circular constellation of stars whirled in front of her, just beyond her reach. Time seemed to slow. She felt Cheshire's hand on the back of her cloak, pulling her away from the curtain. She reached up and undid the feather-shaped clasp around her neck. The cloak fell away from her body, and Dinah stepped inside.

Three

A deep pool of ink encompassed her entire body, only the ink was weightless. As her hands trailed inside it, deep grooves appeared where her fingers had been, lighting up with tiny stars. Constellations swirled around her, and Dinah knew at once everything inside her was made of the same stuff as the stars, that she was light and life and also darkness, capable of swallowing everything around her.

Her feet tipped over her head, and she was yanked upside down, her hair falling away from her face as she swirled in the sky. She kicked a few times before pulling herself hand over hand so that she was right side up—*or was she?* It was hard to tell. Either way, she was climbing, higher or perhaps lower, deeper into the night sky.

As she made her way up—*or down?*—something started happening to the stars around her. There was another crack, and Dinah turned her head to see where it had come from, but there was only the inky blackness and the stars. One after another, the stars plummeted down past Dinah in a shower of sprightly light, each one dancing in their unique constellations. She blinked as everything around her lit up. The inky black shifted to a blinding white light. Effortless beauty tumbled all around her. Her heart felt impenetrable, as if the stars themselves were stitching her wounds closed, wounds shaped by wanting what she could not have.

She understood at once why the curtain had come; it was a warning and a gift. It was a warning of the war that would bring death to so many. The curtain was a warning to those who didn't know that their fates would be forever altered by her fury. It was a gift in that it had bought her a few moments to get her army under control.

Not that it mattered, since she had decided to stay here

in this weightless, twinkling plane. *She would close her eyes, just for a minute, be free from the pain, just for now.*

Something yanked hard at her stomach, and she was pulled backward out of the spinning stars, out of the thick night. Her fingers left streaks of light in the watery black. She flopped backward out of the Sky Curtain and landed hard on the rocky ground below.

"Ow!" she yelped. She tried to stand up, but there was a solid weight pressing down on her chest, so heavy she felt as though her ribs were cracking.

When she opened her eyes, she found herself staring at a dozen ivory spikes, some crusted with dried blood, others so shiny that they reflected her terrified eyes. Morte peered down at her, his massive head inches away from hers. Steam hissed angrily out of his nostrils, singeing the ends of her hair. His lips curled back, and for a moment Dinah thought he might eat her. Instead, a piece of white fabric fell from his lips, landing on her chest. She looked at the fabric. It was from her shirt. Morte had pulled her out of the Sky Curtain.

"I'm here. I'm here," she breathed, reassuring herself and reassuring him.

Cheshire knelt beside her. "Are you all right?"

Dinah looked up at Cheshire, then Morte, who gave a huff and pulled up his massive hoof before bringing it down hard beside her head, a deadly serious reprimand. The ground beneath it cracked under his colossal weight.

Dinah sat up. "I'm fine."

Cheshire stood up with a sigh and smoothed his purple cloak, readjusting his brooch. "She's fine," he muttered to himself. "She'll be the death of me, but she's fine." Then, with a raised eyebrow, he turned and walked away from Dinah.

Sir Gorrann looked at Dinah with fascination. "How did you know to go inside it?"

Dinah shook her head. She couldn't explain. "I just did. How long was I in there?"

Sir Gorrann rubbed his beard. "'Bout a minute's time. We could all see yeh floating there, turning up and down, but it was obvious you couldn't see us." He tilted his head. "What was it like?"

Dinah couldn't explain it, and when she tried, she found

the words all tangled on her tongue. "It was nothing. It was . . . like being free."

She was interrupted by a howl of vicious wind that ripped down from the Sky Curtain, so powerful that it almost blew Sir Gorrann off his feet. The wind ceased, and the curtain stood still for a moment before a single star at the top began falling, cartwheeling through the curtain, hitting other stars on its way down. All the stars began to fall, each one colliding with others in burst after burst of green and yellow light. Everything inside the curtain was falling into brilliant destruction, mirrors of light and swirling blackness appearing at random. Finally, the last star fell, a wispy burst of thin light dropping straight down, as if bent on hurtling itself to its doom. The star disappeared beyond the bottom of the curtain, and then the curtain vanished, as quickly as it came, flickering out like a dying flame.

Dinah looked across the grass, happy to see that the Yurkei were still there, except now they were kneeling, their foreheads pressed against the dirt. Their horses went mad around them. The Spades were either lying or kneeling on the ground. Some covered their heads in fear, some pressed their hands together in prayer, and yet others boasted giddy smiles on their faces.

Sir Gorrann looked at Dinah with amazement. "I believe you've just made yourself a god."

The funeral pyre sparked to life again, gentle crackling sounds filling the air. Smoke began to rise.

"Incredible," breathed Wardley. Dinah closed her eyes at the sound of his voice, at once a balm and a poison.

Yur-Jee and Ki-ershan burst forward from where the curtain had been and practically smothered Dinah, checking her hair and body for wounds.

"I'm all right!" she snapped, gently patting Ki-ershan's arm. She laughed when she saw his bow and arrow drawn. "Did you try to kill it?" Then she noticed a huge pile of arrows on the ground about twenty feet away, on the other side of where the curtain had been. He had indeed. The Yurkei guard's commitment to her life never failed to move her.

The Spades began shouting to each other about what they had just seen.

"Oh gods, just shut it already, you filthy animals! Go to yer tents and stay there!" screamed Starey Belft, reasserting his role as a fearsome Spade commander.

After a moment's pause, the Spades silently obeyed, all anger at the Yurkei defused. The two men who had charged the Yurkei camp left their axes in the dirt and turned away, their heads hanging in shame.

After his troops were in their tents, Starey Belft walked up beside his queen. "What in the bloody hell was that? You're quite the brave one, aren't yeh? Should we call you the Sky Queen?"

He reached his hand down to help Dinah to her feet. It was the first time that he'd truly spoken to her as if she was an equal. She hid her smile by turning away from him.

"Just queen will be fine."

The Spade commander grinned.

With one hand, Dinah reached up for Morte, who lifted his hoof to accommodate her. She slung herself up on his high back, feeling his massive muscles settling themselves against her body. She looked down at her men.

Sir Gorrann's eyes tracked her movement, riveted by

his emboldened leader. "What do you think it meant?"

"It was a warning."

"A warning about what?"

Dinah sat very still. "It was a warning to us, but also about us. War is inevitable."

Sir Gorrann looked out at the Yurkei warriors, still on their knees. The Spades had no idea how close they had come to total obliteration. "They should be warned, just as long as we can keep from killing each other."

♥

Later that evening, as the rest of her army slept, Dinah sharpened her sword beside a fire. A shower of sparks flew down from the blade as she struck it with a rock. Over her shoulder, she felt the creeping presence of someone watching her.

"Hello, Cheshire."

"Hello, daughter." Cheshire turned to Ki-ershan, standing a few feet away from Dinah, so still that he could have been mistaken for a tree in the darkness. "I need a few moments with the queen."

Dinah nodded to Ki-ershan, who took maybe twenty

steps away from them, his glowing blue eyes still visible in the dark night.

Cheshire snickered. "I'll say one thing for the Yurkei, they are quite persistent." He sat down, fanning out his purple cloak so that she'd have a clean and dry spot on the log beside him.

Dinah looked down at the ground while he made himself comfortable. She still wasn't entirely sure how she felt about this man: her father, and yet not at all her father.

"We almost lost the battle today."

"I know." She blinked and lowered her voice. "I know."

"The Sky Curtain must mean that the gods want us to be successful!" he crowed. Then his voice sank back to its normal slithering tone. "Or it wants to save us for destruction at the hands of the king." He shook his head. "This is why I don't believe in the gods."

Dinah looked up. "I don't think it was either of those. I don't know what it meant, I just know how it felt." *It felt like death and life.* "Either way, it's probably the last beautiful thing we will see for a long time."

He nodded thoughtfully before lowering his face so

that it was next to hers. His voice, for once, was gentle. "I watch you, Dinah. I've watched you all my life. I see the dark circles under your eyes. I see the tears you wipe away when you think no one is watching. I see that you are broken." He rested his long fingers on either side of her face. "I know that he rejected you."

Dinah turned away, trying to keep control of her quavering voice. "I don't know what you are talking about."

Cheshire's lips pulled back on his lean face, revealing those hungry white teeth that had so scared her as a child. His grin was wide—wide enough to swallow all of Wonderland. "Don't lie to me, Dinah. After all this time, don't you think I know my own daughter? I can read you like a book." He tucked a piece of her short black hair behind her ear. "My favorite book. A book filled with so much possibility and fire."

She looked away. She much preferred the scheming, genius Cheshire to the kind, fatherly Cheshire. It was obviously quite unnatural for him. Her patient smile faded as her fingertips brushed the tip of her sword. She stuck the tip of the blade into the fire and pulled it out. Its outer ridge glowed orange in the darkness.

"It turns out I have no part to play in Wardley's book. His feelings for me haven't changed. Not since we were children," she whispered finally.

"What has changed in you is the only thing that matters," he said firmly.

Dinah thought about that for a moment. "I'm so angry that he doesn't love me. I'm angry at him, angry at everyone," she whispered. "From when I wake up to the time I close my eyes, it's like a poison underneath my skin. When I see him, I see—" She stopped.

Cheshire leaned over her. "What? What do you see?"

Dinah raised her eyes to his face. "I see rivers of blood," she whispered. Cheshire's face didn't change to the disgusted look that she had been expecting. Instead, a small smile spread across his face.

"Good," he hissed back.

"Good?" Dinah shook her head. "No, that's insanity. Maybe I'm just as crazy as my brother."

"You are nothing like your brother," snapped Cheshire. "He was mad and you are brilliant."

"But the fury . . ."

Cheshire pressed a long fingernail against her heart. "Take that anger, and use it. Use it for battle, use it to rule. Look how you subdued the captain of the Spades today! This anger is a gift, meant to keep you hard. Instead of suppressing it, embrace it. Let it fill your body, your mind, and your heart. It will be your best friend when none are there. Anger is righteousness, it is power, it has made kingdoms and heroes. Without anger, there is no passion, no life."

Dinah sputtered, "But I can't always control it."

Cheshire raised both of his eyebrows, his midnight eyes glittering dangerously in the firelight. "Then don't."

"Once I'm queen . . ."

"Once you are queen, you can deal with Wardley however you see fit. You can marry him, you can kill him, you can make him your boudoir slave."

Dinah made a disgusted sound, but Cheshire continued. "First, you have ten thousand Cards to get through, and a king who wants to see your head mounted outside the gates. Do you not think your anger will serve you well in battle?"

Dinah saw her sword cutting through Card after Card, heart after heart. The excitement of it made the hairs on her arms stand up. If Mundoo knew about her bloodlust . . . She suddenly didn't feel like talking anymore.

"Thank you, Cheshire. I think I'll try to get some sleep now."

Her father stood to leave before looking down at her, his figure impassive in the waning flames. "Dinah, your heart is broken, and it will hurt and fester for years as you yearn for what you cannot have. I know the pain well. Still, you are charged with ruling a nation and uniting a people. These burdens are too heavy for anyone to carry without a fire burning inside of them. Don't try to suppress your beautiful, unruly, angered heart. Let it empower you."

He started to leave but hesitated and added one more thought. He raised his arms, as if scooping up the sky.

"Let it define you."

Four

By the next evening, Dinah's army had reached the outer villages of Wonderland proper. She circled Morte around the settling troops as they nervously unpacked their camp. Dinah's heart hammered quietly in her chest as she looked around. For quite some time, they had seen only the natural, magical places of Wonderland and Hu-Yuhar. Now that she could just make out the buildings on the horizon, Dinah knew there was no turning back. It had been a long time since she had seen buildings of wood, glass, and stone. They

had arrived—Wonderland proper began just over the nearest crag.

The small villages of Wonderland proper held towns-
folk and craftsmen, but mostly farmers. If she squinted, she
could see fields of crops and dewy pink flowers, dotting
the horizon like a blossoming petal stretched thin on the
ground. They were lovely in their overgrown tangle.

Her army proceeded to unpack its gear around her,
and Dinah began assisting her men where they would let
her. What should have taken hours took minutes, and soon
all the Spades and Yurkei settled quietly into their tents on
opposite sides of the field. The sighs of weary men could be
heard as the daylight began to wane. She ordered that the
packs of food be opened, and that each man get twice his
normal amount. The men would eat well tonight. This, at
least, she could give them.

Dinah rode Morte up the neighboring hills, climbing
to where she could see the dilapidated blades of a windmill
creaking in the breeze. She took a deep, terrified breath.
They were on the cusp of battle. Up ahead was Callicarpa,

a small town at the bottom of a low valley, with its famous old windmill marking its farthest northern border. From the town center, plains climbed steadily upward until they encountered a sudden and violent slope down into the meadow that surrounded Wonderland Palace. She stared at the town. It was eerily still. She turned around on Morte to speak to her guards.

"I'm going down to look at Callicarpa. Something seems strange about it."

"No!" snapped Yur-Jee, using his new favorite word. He was still warming up to Dinah. "This not task for queen." He cleared his throat and commanded something in Yurkei.

Before long, Bah-kan rode up beside them, his damp chest hair glistening in the sunlight, his large blade clutched closely against his leg. *It's like seeing a bear ride a horse*, Dinah thought. Even though astride Morte she was several feet taller than he was, Bah-kan leveled his gaze at Dinah. She felt small in comparison.

"Take twelve of your finest warriors ahead to the town. Do not harm or touch anything or anybody. We simply want to see if it will be safe to cross through. Return in less than an hour's time. This is a scouting mission, not an attack."

Bah-kan smiled at Dinah before he galloped down the hill to handpick his men. The Yurkei quickly mounted and soon were stampeding toward Dinah, happy to be doing *something*. She watched silently as the Yurkei whirled past her on their pale steeds, her short hair fluttering in their breezy wake.

"They are so . . . swift," she noted with a smile. She turned to Sir Gorrann, who had ridden up beside her. "How can we train the Spades to move that quickly?"

Sir Gorrann gave a deep laugh. "Oh, my queen. Yeh make me chuckle. There is nothing yeh could do to train those men to move like the Yurkei."

Morte gave an impatient snort and began driving his hooves deep into the ground. He shifted so violently that Dinah was almost pitched from the saddle. It was a long way down, something she knew well.

"What's wrong with yer beast?" asked Sir Gorrann.

"He wants to go." She climbed off him, wincing at the

pain in her shoulder as she gripped the reins above.

"Does that still hurt yeh?" The Spade tilted his head, concerned.

"Not much," she answered, rubbing the sore spot where the chief of the Yurkei had stabbed her with a shallow blade. "It's my daily reminder of Mundoo's long memory."

Sir Gorrann leaned over and rested his hand lightly on her cheek. "And how is yer heart these days? Healing?"

Dinah looked up at him with suddenly blurry black eyes. "That is not your business, sir."

She slapped Morte on his hindquarters and he happily galloped off in the same direction as the Yurkei horses.

"How do you know he'll come back?"

"I don't." Dinah gave a small smile as she began picking wild herbs. She could add them to the scouting party's stew late tonight, one more way to show the men that while she ruled over them, she served them as well. "Morte is not my steed. He is a soldier, under my command, and I am likewise under his command. We are equals."

"And do yeh trust him in battle, Your Majesty? Have you ever seen a Hornhoov in battle?" Sir Gorrann looked down skeptically from Cyndy's back.

"I have not. Well"—she paused—"I did see him kill a white bear."

He dismounted and began helping her set up her tent. Dinah liked being just outside the camp, away from the group. It gave her room to breathe. Slowly, he unfurled the linen flaps that made up the entrance. "Yer father—er, sorry, I mean the king—raided some of the outlying Yurkei territories when yeh were just a babe. During those skirmishes, I saw two Hornhooves in battle. One was Morte. The other one was white and massive, even bigger than he is."

"And?"

"They were utterly *without* mercy. They crushed men like insects under their hooves. Those beasts ran straight into the fold, killing without remorse, even their own men. They would stomp a man to death while impaling another on their bone spikes. I saw a Yurkei spear the white Hornhoov right through the flank, and the beast didn't even flinch. It had arrows sticking out of its *face*. It just kept killing and killing, until someone attempted to sever its head from its body. The Hornhoov killed that man as well, just before its massive head fell from its body."

Dinah could feel the blood draining from her face. "Morte wouldn't . . ."

"He would. I beg of yeh, do not forget his true nature. When yeh bring him into a battle, yer releasing carnage itself. He could kill yeh, and think of how embarrassing it would be to lose yer life to yer own horse just when yer winning the war. Think about that!" He groaned. "Then Cheshire will hurry to set himself as king. Aye, and no one wants that."

Cheshire as king? Dinah had never considered it. Either she would be queen, or she would die, and so would all those loyal to her. The thought that anything else could happen was unnerving.

"What I'm saying, Yer Majesty, is be careful with him. I do not think Morte would ever intentionally hurt yeh, but once he is in the thick of battle, he might not *know* what he's doing."

"I hear what you are saying, Sir Gorrann. Thank you for bringing it to my attention."

Together, they pitted the poles into the ground and

pulled Dinah's tent up. She watched in awe as her black Spade banners curled out on the wind, snapping in the sharp breeze. A talented painter among the Spades had amended the banners to include a red heart, broken down the middle and shifted off center. It was her sigil, same as the one painted on her breastplate. A truer symbol had never been assigned, because her heart was not whole.

Later that evening, Dinah was sitting on a log in front of the tent, looking out in the direction of the palace, when Bah-kan returned with the Yurkei scouting party. The throng of Yurkei warriors surrounded her tent with their pale horses, the men's glowing blue eyes all trained on Dinah. Bah-kan dismounted and walked over to where she sat.

"We searched the village, and the two villages beyond it. They are empty, Your Majesty. Each house and farm has been deserted, stripped of food, weapons, and livestock. We assume that the king has pulled all the villagers inside the palace walls. All available men have most likely been called up to battle." He paused and rubbed his stubbly face. "While this does not bode well for our numbers, it at least guarantees our safety when we march through the villages tomorrow.

There is no danger to be found where there are no enemies."

Dinah thanked the warriors before releasing them to rest for the night. She sent Sir Gorrann to sleep as well, for she needed her loyal Spade at his best when they arrived at the palace. He bowed graciously before kissing Dinah on the forehead. "Sleep well, Queen."

Her favorite Yurkei guard, Ki-ershan, lingered behind and sat down beside her tent, pulling a piece of bread from his bag. "Ji-hoy? How to say it? Uhh . . . roll?" he asked. She nodded. "Roll!" His Wonderlander speech was still broken but improving.

Dinah gladly took the roll and broke it open, releasing the rush of warm honey butter inside. "I'll miss these," she noted as she chewed. "This might be my last taste of Yurkei bread."

Ki-ershan seemed nervous and quieter than normal, and Dinah's curiosity was roused. She nudged him. "Well, out with it."

"Your Majesty . . . I have request of you."

"Yes?"

"I would like to stay with you. As guard, once you are

queen. It would bring me great honor to"—he stumbled over his words—"serve you. I could be a bridge between my people and Wonderland." He gestured out from his chest and then bonded his hands together.

Dinah was touched and laid her hand upon his soft cheek. "Ki-ershan, I would be honored to have you guard me. But are you sure that you don't want to return to Hu-Yuhar? Wonderland Palace is a very different place from your peaceful city. You would feel much less free there, and I can warn you from experience that the life of royalty can sometimes be very dull."

Ki-ershan smiled. "It would not be . . . dull." He tasted the new word on his tongue. "My wife died last year. She had the sickness in Hu-Yuhar. Iu-Hora tried to save her, but he was too late and his potions only eased her pain. She has passed into the sky; her soul rests in the valley of the cranes. Nothing is left for me there. Gye-dohur. *Done.* Protecting you is my life now. I could be translator for the Yurkei."

Dinah gave him a dazzling smile, and he blushed. "That would please me very much. Thank you for honoring me with your request." Dinah gave him a slight nod of her head, but Ki-ershan caught her chin on his finger.

"You may not bow to me. You are queen, and I will bow to you." He awkwardly bowed before her and retreated a few feet to his tent, which was attached to Dinah's. This was more than just mere courtesy—the Yurkei did not bow to Dinah, only to Mundoo, and so Ki-ershan had just committed his life to Dinah as his queen and leader. She found herself deeply moved.

As the night turned late, all the camp was silent. The collective breath of an army of nervous men was more deafening than any sound Dinah had ever heard. She was dressing for bed when her tent flap opened and Cheshire ducked his head through the entrance. She hastily pulled her robe shut, and he turned away awkwardly.

"Your Majesty, I'm sorry to catch you unaware."

"I was just turning in, though I doubt sleep will come. Is something amiss?"

Cheshire pushed his way into her tent, though he was thoroughly uninvited. "Would you like to see the palace?" he whispered. His words caught Dinah off guard.

"What?"

"Come with me. Quietly." She followed him outside, and they both climbed onto his red mare. Ki-ershan and Yur-Jee, always at the ready, shadowed on their horses. In minutes, they had reached the abandoned town. The windows stared at Dinah with their empty, dead eyes. It gave her the feeling of being watched. The horses galloped up a few vistas beyond the abandoned village before coming to the windmill that Dinah could see from her tent. With a grunt, Cheshire shoved open a rickety door to the windmill, his dagger drawn menacingly.

"You don't need that," hissed Dinah. "There is no one in this town."

"You can't be too careful," he answered calmly.

"Wait out here," Dinah instructed the two Yurkei. "We will be right back down."

"I'll go with you, my queen." Ki-ershan dismounted his pale horse and brought up the rear, leaving Yur-Jee outside. Following closely behind Cheshire, Dinah wound up the spiral staircase that led onto the roof. The building smelled of rotting wood and the fetid stench of standing water. The giant heaving windmill blades vibrated through the walls and made a low growl as they spun around the well-worn axle. Once they reached the top, Cheshire seemed to step outside into thin air. Dinah cautiously followed, her feet finding a small ledge lined with a broken railing. She grasped Cheshire's hand and stepped out onto the balcony. A summer wind rippled around them, and Cheshire's plum cloak billowed out from the ledge like a banner. The ledge faced north, and for such a paltry structure, its view was made for a king.

A few villages covered the landscape, black dots on a sea of green-and-yellow grasses. Pale trails of moonlight cast long shadows on the valley, though the pebbled road quietly reflected its light. There were no signs of life in any of the villages. There was nothing to see, with the exception of Wonderland Palace, rising up in the distance, its glorious spires brushing the sky, with the ominous tips of the Black Towers looming behind them.

From there, Dinah could even see the outline of the Royal Apartments, spiraling red-and-white stones that seemed to reach into the heavens. She could just make out the tall iron wall that encircled the castle, the gates that her men would hopefully break open in a day. The palace pulsed with a warm light cast from its thousands of red stained-glass windows. From this balcony, she could even make out the largest heart window, the one that poured its light into the Great Hall. The Great Hall, where the King of Hearts gathered his generals, no doubt preparing to launch his massive defense of the palace. Where he drunkenly laughed at the idea of defeat at the hands of his weak daughter and the Yurkei chief.

"Do you think—"

She didn't get a chance to finish her question. A shadow rose out of the barren village, moving quickly and flying toward them. She opened her mouth to yell, but it was too late. An arrow grazed her cheek and buried itself deep into the mill behind her. When she turned, she could see a red glass heart quivering in its nock.

Dinah leaped back and Ki-ershan shoved past, pushing his torso in front of her and pressing her against the wall behind him. He turned to shield her beneath his arm. Cheshire ducked just as another arrow whistled past his head. His black eyes were wide with fear as he screamed at them both. Two more arrows thunked into the wood above their heads.

"Get the queen inside! Where is that coming from? Ki-ershan? Can you see it?" Ki-ershan, still crouched like a protective animal over Dinah, raised his head.

"There!" He pointed. A small, lone figure was running away from the mill, a bow at his side. Ki-ershan screamed something in Yurkei, and Dinah saw Yur-Jee sprinting after the figure. Dinah's voice was caught in her throat as she watched Yur-Jee quickly gaining on the shadow. Suddenly the Yurkei stopped running, took a deep breath, and raised his bow, a pale arrow nocked on the bowstring.

"Stop!" Dinah cried, but it was too late. In a flash, Yur-Jee released the arrow and it buried itself deep in the figure's back. The small figure pitched forward into the dirt. Ki-ershan grabbed Dinah's arm and yanked her to her feet, pulling her down the rickety stairs. Cheshire, breathing loudly, followed, a dagger clutched to his chest. They ran toward Yur-Jee, who had propped the figure up, his knife at the man's throat. As Dinah approached, her heart sank. It wasn't a man. It was a tall boy, no more than thirteen, pale and wild-eyed. He drew labored breaths that Dinah knew would be his last. A black stain spread rapidly on the front of his shirt. Yur-Jee stepped away and the boy crumpled to the ground.

"Don't go near him," Cheshire warned as they approached. "He's an assassin."

"He's a boy," snapped Dinah. She knelt beside the boy, taking him gently in her arms. He was almost the same age as Charles, but with curly red hair and a generous dotting of freckles. Flecks of blood covered his mouth, and the point of the arrow protruding from his small chest rose and fell with each breath. Dinah laid her hand over the wound and pulled the boy close. His eyes opened and shut at random as he stared at her face. He coughed up blood as he tried to speak.

"Are you the Queen of Hearts?"

Dinah nodded and touched his hair gently. "Why did you do this? Where is your family?" The boy's eyes were fluttering now, and Dinah gave him a soft shake. "Look at me. It's going to be all right. Why did you try to kill me?"

"The king . . . the king . . . he took my family, and he said that if I didn't kill you, he would kill my parents." His unfocused eyes lingered on Dinah's face. "I'm sorry. Please don't . . ." His mouth gave a final tremble, and he pulled himself up to Dinah's ear before resting against her neck. "There is one of us in each village." His body gave a convulsive shake and a raspy rattle passed through his mouth, his sour breath washing over Dinah's cheek.

She looked into his eyes. "I'll protect your family when I am queen. I promise."

A small smile dashed across his face before his cloudy eyes stared out at nothing. His chest stopped heaving. He was gone.

Dinah slowly laid his body down on the ground and used her sleeve to wipe the blood from his mouth. He looked so much like Charles. The same eyes, the same determined mouth. This wasn't an accident. Images of her brother's fractured limbs flooded her mind, of his eyes staring motionless at the stars. She thought of Lucy and Quintrell in a bloody pile, of the dark spot underneath Charles's head, of the crown he made that she would never wear.

Without a word, she stood up and began walking back to camp.

"Your Majesty . . . ," Cheshire called after her.

"Bury him!" she barked in reply.

Cheshire followed her. "He tried to kill you."

Dinah whirled on him. "Only because the king threatened his family! He was innocent, and we buried an arrow in his back." Her shoulders shuddered. "We shot a child."

Cheshire was insistent.

"Yur-Jee could not tell that he was a child. He saw an assassin, one who almost put an arrow through your neck. It is the essence of war, painted in shades of gray that no philosopher could sort out. He tried to kill the queen. We could not let that stand. What if he got away? Made it back to the palace? What if he had been spying on us the entire time?"

Dinah nodded. "I understand your point, Cheshire, but you need to hear mine. I'll not have my army killing children, whatever the circumstances. In the future, anyone who does will answer to me. You and Yur-Jee will bury the child. With your hands."

Cheshire's eyes darkened. "Watch your tone, daughter, lest you forget who you fight. In two days, we will march on the palace, and there will be no mercy for any of us. Remind yourself why you lead this army and steel your dark heart. There is more blood ahead than you could imagine."

Cheshire turned, but Dinah grabbed his arm. "My dark heart beats just fine," she snapped before letting go. "And it's big enough to sustain my rage *and* my mercy."

Cheshire stared at her for a long moment before dropping his head. "If you say so. If it is your wish, I will help bury the child."

Dinah held his gaze. "Good."

She was left alone, huddled in the dark, as the men worked nearby to bury the ginger-haired boy. Her hands and neck were covered with slick blood that she frantically tried to wipe on the dried grass at her feet. It wouldn't come off. Dinah raised her hands to the moonlight, illuminating her wet palms. *A queen's hands*, she told herself.

Hands trembling, she pushed herself to her feet and raised her weary head. *I am the queen*, she told herself over and over again until she felt it thrumming through her body, hoping it would stiffen her resolve. Behind her, she could hear the sounds of earth showering down onto the boy's body, the child resting forever in the cool ground. She stared in the direction of the palace. Her tears dried on her cheeks. She let Cheshire's advice wash over her.

She would let the fury define her, not the mercy. It was too painful.

"I am coming *for you*," she whispered to the night air, to the King of Hearts, a man who made a habit of killing children. She rested her hand on her sword as she let her rage writhe through her veins. There were no stars that night, for even they trembled at what lay before them.

Q
♥

Five

Dawn came early on the morning of battle, marked by a light rain that gently peppered the ground. The weather seemed to agree that this forlorn day had finally arrived. The rain fell lightly on her tent, making a lulling sound. Dinah lay still and concentrated on not opening her eyes. She knew that once she opened them, it would begin. By nightfall, her fate would be determined—either she would sit proud and triumphant upon the Heart throne, or she would be buried in the wet Wonderland earth, forever scorned as a traitor to her people.

Every day since she had left the palace, Dinah opened her eyes with the expectation that she might die. Still, today was different. Today death was not an unknown figure whispering between the trees. Today she would challenge death to a duel, a game in which the odds lay against her in spades. A hysterical laughter bubbled out of her, a mad laugh that made her sound just like Charles. *In Spades.* Her calloused hands trembled under her thin blanket.

It was the image of his broken body that finally forced open her black eyes, awash in tears. She stared at the roof of the tent, listening to the sounds of her army outside. Finally, Dinah rose slowly and washed her face in a basin of ice-cold water. A tray of hearty food had been left out for her—by Wardley, probably. Her stomach was knotted so tightly that it hurt to breathe. She forced herself to shove down a few eggs and a crust of bread. *It would have to do.*

For a few moments, she sat silently on the edge of her cot, staring through a small hole in her tent at the naked plains of Wonderland, dotted with black Spades and painted Yurkei horses.

"I am the queen," she whispered to herself. She tried

repeating the phrase over and over again, but her words faltered, tangled up inside her throat, caught in a knot of fear. She was staring at herself in the looking glass when Sir Gorrann poked his head through the tent flap.

"It's time, Yer Majesty."

Dinah looked up at the Spade, brave and powerful in his shining black armor.

"Dinah?"

"I'm afraid," she whispered.

He knelt before her, his armor clanking against the ground as he took her hands in his and laid his forehead against her palm. "Everyone is afraid before a battle. No one speaks of the fear, though. Yeh cannot give it a name, for when yeh do, it becomes real. The Spades, Cheshire, the Yurkei, Mundoo, all those Cards that line the iron gates, all the people inside the palace grounds, and even the king himself—each one woke up today with the fear, deep inside of here." He gently laid his hand over Dinah's heart. "Even so, yeh will lead us into battle today, as a symbol of change. Yeh stand before Wonderland's gates today as the rightful queen, an heir to yer mother's line. And lastly, yeh stand before the King of Hearts today as a symbol of vengeance and justice, for the murder of yer brother, for Faina Baker, for my family, for the thousands of Yurkei, and for the innocent people of Wonderland he has murdered or imprisoned. We all must stand eventually, even if our knees shake."

Dinah bent forward and kissed him on the forehead. "Thank you," she whispered. "For everything."

He left her alone, but just seconds later her tent flap opened once again, this time revealing a couple of Yurkei warriors who had come to dress her. Dinah stood with her arms outstretched as the Yurkei silently applied white stripes of paint to her arms and legs before wrapping them in a fine cloth dipped in Iu-Hora's medicine to ward off infections. Over that, she was dressed in a simple white tunic and black wool pants before her armor was fastened around her. First came the breastplate, bright white with a broken red heart painted across it. It hit her at the hip, its edge sharp with tiny red hearts. The Yurkei gingerly lifted her legs as she stepped into her heart-covered, black leather leg guards that rose up the thigh. Red leather straps were added to protect her hips and shoulders. When they finished draping her body with the heavy armor, the warriors left the tent abruptly, without warning. She flexed her legs. The armor was heavy, but she was able to move fairly smoothly.

She heard quiet, purposeful steps, and Dinah looked up as Cheshire walked into the tent carrying her cape. He carefully draped it on her and then gently latched it at her neck. The white crane feathers, each appearing as if they had been dipped in blood, circled her, the cape's weight brushing the floor while at the same time stretching out behind her like wings.

Cheshire stepped back and sighed, his eyes filling with tears. "Oh, my fierce warrior. For once, I am speechless. Look at yourself."

She turned to the mirror. Dinah's eyes widened in surprise as she barely recognized herself. A grown woman, proud and strong, stared at her, her eyes simmering like two burning coals, her pitch-black hair falling just below her chin. Cheshire reached for her crown.

"No," said Dinah. "I'll do it." Watching herself in the mirror, she lifted the thin ruby crown and pushed it down onto her head. It sat snugly, a perfect fit. She looked at herself.

This woman does not need fear, she thought. *She is a queen.*

"I'm ready."

"You are a terrifying vision of glory," Cheshire noted, with a sly smile. "Let's hope the King of Hearts thinks so." Just before she stepped outside, Cheshire spun her to face him. "Dinah, do not forget the plan. Even if you see the king, do not pursue him. There will be a time for your justice, and Charles's justice, but now is a time for battle. If you go galloping off after the king on the north side, everything will descend into chaos. . . ."

Dinah nodded. "I won't. I'll follow the plan."

His dark eyes bore into hers. "The plan is perfect. All you have to do now is fight. Let that anger rise. We are all behind you." He bowed his head. "Your army awaits."

With a deep breath, Dinah straightened her shoulders and stepped outside the tent. She heard a collective gasp and then found herself too moved to speak. At the bottom of the hill, Spade and Yurkei stood together for the first time. They lined the walkway from her tent to Morte, who waited for her at the end of a long column of men, his reins held gently by Sir Gorrann. Wardley, devastatingly handsome in his silver armor, stepped up beside her and raised his hands to cup his mouth. The crowd fell silent.

"All hail the Queen of Hearts!"

Dinah began walking slowly toward Morte, her cape dancing over the wet grass. As she moved past them, each man and warrior bowed before her, falling to their knees in ardent devotion. The rhythm of their falling heads reminded her of the Ninth Sea, a gentle washing of movement. Dinah held her head high, her face a stony mask of determination. The Spades extended their hands to her, and she made sure she brushed each reaching hand with her own. She was grateful and overwhelmed at their devotion, and even more so by this staggering show of loyalty from the Yurkei. For today, she was their chief. They would not bow before her tomorrow.

At the end of the aisle stood Morte, equal parts splendid and monstrous in his armor, which the Yurkei had designed for him. His wide flanks and chest were protected with black armor, painted with the same red heart that Dinah carried on her breast. The rest of his body had been striped with white paint. The bone spikes around his hooves were polished gleaming white, their sharp tips reflecting the light. *Gods, he was terrifying.* His mouth was open and salivating, the Hornhoov hungry for the coming battle. Dinah's new saddle sat snug against his neck, and when she approached him, he lifted his leg for her. With a smile, she stepped onto the bony spikes and felt the familiar sensation of being flung onto his high back. She settled into the saddle and looked at the wide road ahead—the road that led to the palace. Morte pawed the ground with anticipation, and Dinah wheeled him around to face her kneeling troops. There was a moment of silence as they stared at their queen, a vision of fury and power. She cleared her throat and raised her voice over the plains.

"Will you join me, my friends and men? Will you march to Wonderland Palace beside me?" Their roar shook the ground and rattled the walls of Dinah's heart. She smiled. "The king waits for us. Let us go and meet him!"

♥

It took them over two hours to reach the palace, and another hour to climb the hill that Cheshire had pointed out so many times on the wooden Wonderland map. By then, the sun had made its appearance and blazed down on a scene that it would not soon forget.

Outside the circular gates of Wonderland Palace, bordering every inch of the thirty-foot iron walls, were Cards. In some places they were a hundred deep, lined shoulder to shoulder, more people than Dinah had ever seen in one place. The Cards were thickest on the north side, where they were already facing the impassive line of Mundoo's army. The mounted Heart Cards that lined the north side clearly outnumbered the Yurkei army two to one. *But*, she thought, *each Yurkei warrior is as strong as three regular men.*

The banners of the Hearts, Diamonds, and Clubs flapped in the wind above hundreds of archers looking down from the turrets of the palace. Some of them were of the infamous Fergal family, no doubt, deadly and accurate with their arrows.

A stray Spade wandered up next to Dinah. "Wha' are they waiting for?" He stared down at Mundoo's unmoving forces.

Dinah's eyes never left the palace. "Us. They are waiting for us. Now get back in line."

"'Course, my queen."

On the south side of the palace, where they waited for Dinah's army, hordes of Diamonds, Clubs, and a handful of Heart Cards all jeered and shouted, hungry for battle. Cheshire had been perfect in his calculations: the skilled fighters were on the north side, the brutes on the south. Stretching all the way around the palace, the king's men stood in a perfect circle, thousands more than Dinah had anticipated. In his fear, he had left no man, no resource, unturned.

The Heart Cards on the north side stood fearless, their swords drawn and ready, their red-and-white uniforms glinting brightly in the sunlight. Facing Dinah on the south side, holding every manner of hideous weapon, Clubs grunted and pounded their chests. Beside each Club, chained together in a line, stood strings of men, each armed with a single knife. *Prisoners*, thought Dinah, looking down, her hand tangled in Morte's mane. Just as Wardley had predicted, her father had emptied the Black Towers to enlist more men for the battle. The men looked terrified; they squinted in the sunlight, unable to properly see from their time in the darkness. With chains around their wrists, those men didn't have a prayer. One Spade would be able to kill the lot of them.

More daunting than the Clubs were the large clusters of Diamond Cards, their purple cloaks a bright splash of color in the sea of black, white, and red. Standing perfectly still, they tossed their daggers back and forth between themselves without even turning their heads. They moved like a constellation, with a sharp, deadly bite. Above their heads, turrets had been assembled for the archers to peer down from, their bows aimed directly at her men. Bah-kan rode up beside her.

"You ready?" he asked Dinah.

Strangely, the answer slipped out simply, without thought or fear.

"I'm ready."

A cheer rose up from Mundoo's army, which had completely encircled the palace. She watched as the Yurkei erupted with excitement, a rocking mass of terrifying sounds, all striped white and astride their pale steeds. Mundoo was riding Keres near the front, dressed from head to toe in blue and white feathers. From the back of his steed, with his huge sword drawn, he screamed instructions at his army. Their wild cries reached the Yurkei who waited behind Dinah, and they responded with yelps of their own. The two armies were ready, and soon they would smash against Wonderland from both sides, a furious attack not even her father could have imagined.

From her vantage point on the hill, she watched as the north palace gates opened and the king emerged, surrounded by a thick swarm of mounted Heart Cards. He straddled his own white Hornhoov, his red armor glinting in the light, his Heartsword raised above his head. The Cards erupted in cheers, showering down roses from their outstretched hands. The king's Hornhoov trampled the delicate flowers underfoot. A group of men suddenly broke from his side and began galloping around the outskirts of the palace.

Dinah's heart clenched, and she heard Wardley, who had sidled up beside her, mutter to himself. Xavier Juflee, the Knave of Hearts, was now riding toward the south side with a large group of Heart Cards. Wardley's old mentor was the most skilled fighter in all of Wonderland, and he would cut through the Spades (and most of the Yurkei) with deadly ease.

"Damn him," muttered Wardley behind her. "Gods damn him."

There was a moment of silence while the king's and Mundoo's armies stared at each other. All the way around the palace, the Cards stood perfectly still and disciplined, waiting for one of the two opposing armies to make a move. Silence permeated the air. Finally, one of the Spades began stomping his feet and clanking his sword against his shield. The other Spades followed. Soon, the two thousand men lined up behind her began bellowing and shaking their swords at the Cards. The Yurkei made calling sounds that resonated within their throats. The Spades joined in, their voices rising and falling like thunder over the open ground. It was the sound of a united army, and it filled Dinah's heart with a fierce desire to protect them.

Bah-kan climbed off his steed, a bundled package in his outstretched hand. Gingerly, he unwrapped a single white arrow, elaborate carvings covering its abnormally large head, and nocked it into his bow. Every eye on the south side of Wonderland Palace watched in silence as he pointed the bow into the sky and released the arrow. It climbed higher than any arrow Dinah had ever seen. Once the shaft reached the apogee of its trajectory, it exploded into a streaming trail of shimmering gold that draped the palace, such a lovely sight to start an ugly war. The arrow was the signal; Dinah's small army was ready, and Mundoo could make his advance.

Morte began to buck underneath Dinah, anxious to run into the fight.

Wardley rode up beside her and looked at Morte with doubt. "Are you sure you don't want to ride with me?"

Dinah didn't answer, her eyes trained on the army awaiting her. Sir Gorrann, Starey Belft, Bah-kan, and Cheshire rode up behind her now, their heads bowed in reverent silence. It was time. Ki-ershan brought his steed up beside Dinah, with Yur-Jee flanking her other side.

"Your Majesty." Yur-Jee gave her a wide smile, the first Dinah had ever seen from him. He hit his chest. "READY!"

Dinah let her eyes linger over the dear men who fought for her crown, their faces so determined, each man silently praying to the Wonderland gods. Only Cheshire looked unbothered. In fact, he looked downright bored. A small smile crept across her face. *Of course Cheshire would be bored.*

The sound of trumpets filled the air, blasting their deafening cacophony from the palace. Dinah felt the sound deep within her, traveling up through her lungs to the tips of her fingernails. *It has begun*, she thought.

On the opposite side of the palace, Mundoo proudly rode a swiftly galloping Keres, his hands meeting together over his head in the symbol of the crane. His army grew silent as they remembered those who had gone before them into the valley of the cranes. Then he turned, straight for the Heart Cards, and drew his sword. With loud whoops, Mundoo's troops began galloping wildly toward the king and his Cards. Morte's haunches gave a violent jerk and the ground beneath him began to rumble, as if it were opening up.

"Steady," she breathed. "Steady. We have to wait."

The sound of sixteen thousand hooves filled the air, shaking the ground, and a collective roar from the Cards below answered back as they pointed their weapons.

The King of Hearts waited patiently for them to arrive, his Heartsword held tight, his arm outstretched to signal the archers. Mundoo's army continued its charge. The archers on the north turrets raised their arrows. All of Wonderland held its breath. Then, at the king's dropped hand, the Wonderland archers unleashed a sky's worth of dark arrows, each one tipped with a red glass heart. The arrows climbed mercilessly into the sky before their heads pointed downward and began their descent onto the galloping Yurkei warriors. Dinah's breath caught in her throat as the bright red shower of death raced toward them.

Mundoo gave a shout, and at his command, each Yurkei warrior reached down to untie a white bag that had been lashed to his saddle. Mundoo gave a final cry, and the Yurkei warriors ripped open their bags, just as the arrows began raining down upon them. Thousands of huge white cranes launched themselves from the bags, happy to be free. The cranes appeared in the sky as a great white cloud hovering over the Yurkei, a cluster of white wings so thick that for a moment, Dinah couldn't even see the Yurkei army. The arrows destined for the Yurkei buried themselves in the birds and littered the ground around them, a sea of white and red. The surviving cranes flapped and screamed, now defensive of their tribe, swooping down and creating chaos among the mounted Heart Cards, plucking weapons from their hands and impaling eyes with their long beaks. Once the cloud of cranes had lifted from above the Yurkei, Dinah saw that in those few moments, all the Yurkei had drawn their bows.

The Wonderland archers never knew what hit them. A flurry of arrows buried themselves in the heart, eye, or head of each one. *The Yurkei never missed.* Screams of pain echoed through the valley, and Dinah saw men falling from the towers. Swifter than she had ever believed possible, the Yurkei reloaded their bows and sent their second barrage of arrows straight into the line of mounted Heart Cards now riding toward them. Their horses screamed and buckled as their riders fell.

Mundoo and Keres pulled ahead and ran straight past the king into the line, followed by four thousand Yurkei warriors. The king turned his Hornhoov and followed him into the fray. From there, it was hard to make out what was happening. The two lines of horses broke against each other, and the mounted Yurkei swarmed over the Cards like a crashing wave. The sounds of war—gut-wrenching screams of metal on metal, shrieks of pain, cheers of victorious combatants, and the last gasps of the dying—echoed from the valley.

Dinah turned her eyes toward the army that awaited them. The Cards on the south side had obviously heard Mundoo's advance and the sounds of agony echoing from the other side of the palace. The line that earlier had stood as still as statues was now agitated and nervous. The Cards were talking to one another: "What are they waiting for?"

We will hold, she thought, *we will hold until your minds break*. She realized too late that it wasn't she who would make the decision of when they advanced. Morte was prancing and smashing his hooves into the earth so violently Dinah could barely stay on him. If Morte bolted, she would arrive first at the line, without an army behind her. That couldn't happen. She held him as long as she could, and when she felt that his patience was wearing thin, she turned back to her army, trying desperately to memorize each face of the men who fought for her. Her eyes found Sir Gorrann, who gave her a strong nod. Shakily, she stood in her saddle. Morte realized the gravity of the moment and for once stood perfectly still, his head raised with pride. As Dinah stood, the Spades raised their weapons in a show of unity, and the Yurkei lifted their hands, making the sign of the crane.

Dinah raised her voice to be heard over the terrible sounds of battle below. "My loyal army! You were once enemies, and today you stand united against a fearful and weak king. Today your names will be entered into Wonderland's history books, and someday you will tell your children about the morning that changed everything." The Spades erupted in wild cheers. "Today we will take back what is rightfully ours, be it our land, or rights"—she paused—"or a crown!"

The army erupted in deafening roars, and the sound of their swords clanging together rose over the plains.

"Fight today not for yourselves, but for every prisoner in the Black Towers, for every Spade never able to take a wife, for every Yurkei who lost his land to a greedy line of kings! Fight today for them, fight today for me!"

She paused and drew her finger dramatically across her neck.

"Off with their heads!"

The army answered back, "*Off with their heads!*"

The entire army was flooding toward her now, spurred on by her speech. Dinah turned Morte, holding his red leather reins as tightly as possible. He bucked and kicked, angry that he had not been unleashed as the rest of the horses flew past them. Wardley brought Corning up beside her, their silver armor blazing like a million suns.

"Dinah . . ." His voice washed over the walls she built in her heart to keep him out. She was powerless before him. She turned her head to meet his gaze. There was nothing else she could do, no lie she could tell. She stared unflinchingly into his eyes.

"Wardley, I love you. I always have and I always will." She was not seeking the reply she would never hear; rather it was something she needed him to know. He gave her a sad smile that broke her heart all over again.

"I know, Dinah. And with the gods as my witnesses, I will die beside you today or see you crowned queen."

Wardley held out his hand and she took it, lacing their fingers together. Together they stood for a moment as the Yurkei warriors rushed past them, two childhood friends whose lives had brought them somewhere unimaginable. He gave her hand a squeeze before releasing it. "Clear the path to the gates, and then retreat. Do you hear me?"

Dinah nodded and turned Morte in the direction of the

palace. She could barely contain him now. A path had opened up before them, with Spades running past on either side.

"Try not to leave us too far behind," yelled Ki-ershan, who was already getting a head start, galloping as fast as he could toward the palace. Sir Gorrann and Wardley began moving their horses toward the line of Cards as well, getting as far out ahead of Dinah as they could.

Sir Gorrann was screaming at her over the deafening noise. "Hold him! Hold him back!"

Morte's body gave a violent jerk, and then another. Dinah held on to him, but it was like trying to hold a wave back from the shore with a simple leather strap. He was bucking and leaping so violently that Dinah's arm cracked against his neck.

He was trying to buck her off. *She was torturing him*, she could feel that now. She could not contain his fury, any more than she could contain her own. Finally, she opened her eyes and faced the palace, taking just one deep breath. The Queen of Hearts released the reins.

"Go."

Six

Morte shot forward, leaving clouds of dust behind his hooves. Together they were flying, his spiked hooves meeting the ground with immeasurable force. Dinah pressed hard against his neck. Within seconds, she passed Cheshire, then easily overtook Wardley and Sir Gorrann. The army of running Spades watched in amazement as they flew past, a black blur of physical power and fury. Dinah heard the cheers of the mounted Yurkei rise around her as she dashed by them toward the line of Cards, their shields raised and trembling as death itself thundered down on them.

The king's Cards were prepared for a strike at the very front of the line, assuming that the enemy would penetrate their forces that way. And yet, as the Cards watched in horror, the front line of Dinah's forces slowed and began to change shape as they grew closer. At her shout, the front line pulled back and the sides expanded in a wide half circle that flanked the castle. They reached around both sides and when it seemed they could stretch no longer, they met with Mundoo's forces in the middle. The armies were merged, and they swallowed the Cards like a gaping, hungry mouth.

The Cards were taken by surprise and pressed close to each other in shock and fear. She was almost upon them now, and Morte showed no signs of stopping. *I must clear a path to the gates*, she thought. The Cards positioned their spears and swords as she approached, as if they were facing a normal steed. One of the soldiers in the front carried a mirrored shield, and just before they collided with the Cards, Dinah saw a distorted reflection of herself. Faina Baker's words played in her mind.

Straddle the devil. . . .

Suddenly Dinah remembered Iu-Hora's words to her

that day in the tent filled with blue smoke.

Queen of Hearts, the daughter of two fathers, heed my words. You will pierce the heart of one man and cut out the heart of the one you love most. Follow the crumbs to find your throne and only then shall your head rest in the grass.

She blinked, the sweat running into her eyes. Did that mean she would die today? She almost didn't care. Her senses heightened. Dinah could hear the men breathing, shouting. She smelled them, that pungent smell of fear and bloodlust that she, the Queen of Hearts, was causing. With a wicked smile, she opened up her heart and mind, letting the black rage that she constantly suppressed climb up her chest and flood her body. She allowed it to overtake her, its fiery taste seductive on her tongue. It tasted like blood. Seconds before entering the fray, she leaned forward and whispered three simple words to Morte: *"Kill them all."* His body surged beneath her.

There was no time to draw her sword. She simply clung as tightly as she could to his neck and held on. The sound of Morte hitting the line was something she knew she would never forget—high-pitched screams, metal on bone, the ripping of flesh, the wail Morte released as he flew over the spears and into a throng of men pushing at him with swords and clubs.

Frothing at the mouth, he joyfully began striking out with his hooves as Dinah grasped him with all her strength. Without flinching, he trampled the two men in front of him, his huge hooves cracking their skulls and crushing their faces into pulp that burst against the ground. One man was impaled on his back hoof, and Morte stamped him again and again until his feet were free, leaving the man in pieces. Rising up on his hind legs, he spun and brought his crushing feet down upon three more men. He kicked a Club straight in the face, and when Dinah looked back, the man was faceless.

There was chaos all around her. Morte, covered in blood, ripped a man's jaw from his face with his teeth. Sir Gorrann, beside her, plunged his sword straight through a Heart Card's chest. The man fell off his horse, his blood pooling around him. His eyes rested momentarily on Dinah before he passed into the beyond. Dinah recognized him—he had been one of her palace guards. The sight shook her back to reality.

An arrow whizzed past her head, and then another. She ducked and reached for her shield attached to Morte's side, holding it above her head for protection. Morte spun around, trying to avoid the arrows that suddenly were raining down all around them. One pierced his ear and he let out a loud scream before plunging his front hoof into the chin of a Yurkei warrior. The warrior slumped against it, his bright blue eyes open in confusion as Morte tried to shake him off.

A Heart Card tried to grab Dinah's leg and pull her off Morte. Dinah kicked him twice in the mouth, knocking out a few teeth before he fell away. From the corner of her eye, she saw a Club stalking toward her, his uniform peppered with medals, an ax held aloft in his hand, his eyes only on Dinah. Morte let out a scream and reared back. When he lifted his feet off the ground, Dinah drew her sword. It slid from her sheath, and she relished its weight in her hand. She felt alive, each pore and vein flooded with an ecstasy she had never known. She felt immortal, powerful, and rash. *She would bring death upon these men.*

Morte landed hard, jostling the saddle loose as the ground around him shuddered. The Club with the ax was almost upon them. Dinah pulled Morte back, barely escaping the edge of the Card's weapon as he swung forward. Morte spun and knocked the man sideways with his flank, and before he could rise, Dinah shoved her sword deep into the Club's throat, the tip of the blade poking out from the back of his neck. He looked up at her in shock, and Dinah's eyes took in his surprised face. He slumped forward against her steed. Dinah pulled her sword, slick with blood, from his body before kicking his still form to the side. She smiled winsomely, and then turned to kill another.

Pushing toward the gate, Morte brought his hooves down onto two Diamond Cards who silently appeared before him, but not before one of them buried his dagger deep in Morte's shoulder. Morte didn't seem to notice, even as Dinah yanked the dagger out of him. She sent it deep into the eye of a young Heart Card who ran toward her with his sword drawn. He fell facedown in a rush of dark blood.

An arrow struck the breastplate just above her heart with a loud thunk, and Dinah looked up to see two archers running toward her. There was nowhere to hide, and she struggled to turn Morte away from them. They nocked arrows into their bows and Dinah raised her shield, afraid but unwavering, waiting for the pain to begin.

As an elaborate dance of men and blood swirled around them, Yur-Jee appeared next to her, sank to his knees, and fired two arrows from his pale bow. The approaching archers fell in perfect symmetry, arrows through their necks. Before Yur-Jee could turn away, a Heart Card ran up behind him and, smiling widely, slit his throat. Dinah screamed in horror as Yur-Jee struggled to breathe and then left this world behind, his bright blue eyes dulling to gray as he stared at the sky.

The Heart Card smiled at Dinah before lunging toward her. Dinah clipped his ear off with her sword. Morte crushed his body under the weight of his hooves, the man's torso caving in like a dropped melon.

A wide circle cleared around Morte. In those few seconds, Dinah was able to assess what was happening: her forces were pushing the king's Cards back toward the iron gates, where they were being massacred in large numbers by the Yurkei warriors.

Loud screams erupted to her right, and Dinah turned

to see several of her men running, their limbs engulfed in black flame. The king's archers were unleashing burning sticks of nightpowder, the flames that blazed without smoke. The screams of the burning men echoed over the battlefield. Dinah was about to turn Morte in that direction when, without warning, hundreds of the remaining cranes descended on the archers, pulling them up and over the turrets, dropping them onto the ground below.

Dinah wiped the sweat from her eyes as Morte darted forward into a bunch of Cards. She brought down her sword on heads, on arms, and on hands. She lost track of time. In the moment, it was impossible to tell who was winning, and many times Dinah caught herself almost attacking one of her Spades. It was the chaos of war, the sides gradually blending together. It was terrible and wonderful, the fear of death and the rush of power equally tingling through her system after she pulled her sword from body after body.

Dinah raised herself from the saddle, just enough to see her position. The Yurkei were moving swiftly through the crowd, and she spotted a large group of bloodied Spades pushing their way through the opening that Morte had cleared to the gates, protected by battered shields on every side.

She saw men and boys dying around her, the pleas of mercy falling on deaf ears. Some were shown it, others were not. *What had her wrath wrought?* She continued to push Morte toward the gate.

A large Club Card emerged from under the slumped bodies of two Yurkei beside her, catching Morte off guard. He violently lurched sideways into the man, but the Club, unnaturally tall, swung his weapon square into her torso, catching Dinah in the stomach and breastplate. Before she had time to react, she was hurled backward off Morte. It was a long fall to the ground. She landed heavily on her hip, and the armor that was supposed to protect her pushed all the air from her lungs. Her sword spun away.

She could feel blood leaking out of her side. Was she cut? Impaled? Her heavy feather cape swirled around her, the blood that dotted the feathers now included some of her own. She gasped for breath, once, twice, but couldn't get air.

Move! she told herself, crawling toward her sword. *Move!* Morte's hooves were coming down all around her, and for a moment she feared only him as she lay in the dirt, hands over her head.

Unaware Dinah was gone in the midst of his battle fervor, Morte whirled and galloped in the direction of a group of particularly nasty Diamond Cards who were sending daggers through every Yurkei that came their way. When he barreled through them, their screams vibrated in her ears. Crawling through the bloody mud, Dinah reached her sword and lifted it just in time to impale a wounded Heart Card, his sword raised to strike her. His weight swallowed the sword through his body as he fell, and Dinah struggled to pull it free from his rib cage.

Without warning, a chain-mail glove caught her on the temple, and Dinah fell sideways, away from her weapon. Her ears rang as she struggled to stay conscious. She blinked twice before pushing up to her knees, her hand reaching for the dagger in her boot. The man was on her at once. They scrambled on the ground, his sweaty face pressed up against hers, his hands tangled in her hair and her crown. Her eyes widened when his face came into focus. It was Yoous, the giant Club who had escorted them through the Black Towers.

"Well, hello, Princess. Fancy meeting you here." His sour breath washed over her face, his smile wide. "Thought you made a fool of me, did you? Well, when I bring your head to the king, I'll make sure that it has a special place in the Black Towers, somewhere I can see it every day." He yanked her up by her hair as Dinah flailed and struggled. His blade poked into her throat, a trickle of blood dampening her collar.

Dinah jabbed her elbow sharply into his stomach and he gasped. She tried to spin away from him, but he stepped on the edge of her cape and pulled her body close to his. His rough hands angled her chin to look at his face, his sword held firmly against her breast. "Take your last breath, my lady. I'll never see a wench like you as my—"

There was a gurgling sound, and suddenly Yoous's head was separated from his shoulders. Dinah looked up in shock and relief as she saw Wardley emerge through the red mist, his entire armor streaked with blood, a nasty open wound on his cheek. He clasped his arms around her waist. She slumped against him. Together they ran through the fighting hordes of rabid men.

"Wait! Morte!" she cried.

"We can't help him! He's gone!"

They ran into two Clubs, and Wardley dispatched one easily enough, while Dinah plunged her recovered sword through the remaining Card's thigh. To her right, she saw a Diamond Card raise his hand to throw his dagger at Wardley, but in the second that he measured his aim, she buried her own dagger in his neck. His eyes went wide with surprise before he fell facedown into the ground.

With a cry, Dinah ripped the cape off from around her neck and leaped free of its weight, her sword out in front of her. She beckoned to the Cards who approached.

She fought in time with Wardley now, a mirror image of the dance they had perfected years ago. Only this time, it wasn't a game. Fighting for their lives, they slashed through the men as they moved through the crowd toward Corning, who was whinnying for his master, two arrows poking out of his flank.

They had almost made it to him when Dinah heard a strange grinding sound, like chains being dragged over stony ground. The sound chugged slowly up the palace wall and echoed off the turrets, the high-pitched ringing deafening to all below.

"The Jabberwocky!" screamed Wardley. "*Move!*"

Together, they ran as quickly as they could. Dinah heard the whistling overhead and increased her speed, her lungs and side aching with each raw breath.

"Get down!" Wardley screamed at his men as he ran. "Get down, swords up!"

Wardley slammed to a stop and pulled Dinah beside him. She could see that they were safely out of range, but almost worse, they could now watch the Jabberwocky inflict its carnage.

The weapon came spinning out from behind one of the turrets, vaulted from a catapult inside the walls of the palace. Dinah watched as the whirling thirty-foot iron sphere was launched over the walls and spun faster and faster, gaining speed as it hurtled down on Cards and Yurkei alike. Wardley was screaming and Dinah joined him, their voices easily lost in the cacophony of battle. She watched in horror as it untangled, wider and wider, until its true form took shape: a large net made of crumpled metal, covered with curled iron spikes. It soared high into the air before it began its plummet toward the ground, its gigantic width encompassing a quarter of the battlefield. Men ran, screaming, but it was too late. The Jabberwocky careened down from the sky like a metal blanket.

♥

Oh gods.

"Get down! Swords up!" Dinah's eyes found Sir Gorrann, just as he finished off a decorated Heart Card. "Get down!" she screamed, waving her arms frantically. He looked up just in time to see an agonizing death hurtling toward him. The Spade curled himself into a small ball and pointed his sword at the sky. Starey Belft was running toward a large group of Spades, screaming and waving to warn them. But he was too late.

The Jabberwocky landed with an earth-shattering *crack*, its metal netting covering hundreds of bodies. Its curved hooks pinned its victims to the ground like insects on a board.

Screams of agony rang out over the plains as the king's weapon took limbs, eyes, shoulders, mouths. Silence fell over the battlefield as everyone stared at the spot where the men had been, now just a quivering mass of metal. Seconds passed and Dinah didn't breathe, not until several swords popped up from below, sawing through the metal. The few men who had knelt with their swords or shields protecting them from the Jabberwocky's terrible claws emerged. Through the holes they had made, Dinah saw glimpses of terrible suffering—men impaled, their lifeless eyes staring up in shock. A pool of blood crept out from under the net now, and Dinah looked away, but not before she saw Sir Gorrann shake himself off and head back into the fray. Her heart resumed beating. Starey Belft, commander of the Spades, did not emerge. He was gone.

The cranking sound filled the air again, but more dimly this time.

"They're sending one out on the other side!" Wardley

yelled, plunging his sword into the heart of a suffering Yurkei, a mercy killing. Dinah's face was wet with tears. Her army was decimated. At least half of them were dead or dying, though the king's army was worse off. Loud screams echoed from the other side of the palace as the second Jabberwocky ended thousands of lives in its metal tangle of death.

Her misguided attention was noticed, and two Heart Cards abruptly grabbed her arms, dragging her backward. Dinah spun out of their grasp. Wardley tackled the other man, pressing him to the ground and throttling him. The Card quickly lost consciousness. Dinah sparred with the man she'd disarmed, her blade moving faster and faster with each stroke. Finally, the man raised his arm a little too high. She plunged her sword into his stomach, through his thin leather armor.

Before she could even pull her sword free, another Diamond Card grabbed at her, latching onto her breastplate, and hurled her to the ground. Dinah pushed herself backward while the Diamond advanced on her, an amethyst-encrusted dagger in his hand. The Card raised his arm, his eyes trained on Dinah's face.

Without so much as a whisper, Ki-ershan leaped on the man's back, his white-striped hands wrapped around the Card's neck. He gave a jerk and the man's head twisted abruptly with a sickening crack. He fell lifelessly to the ground. Ki-ershan yanked Dinah to her feet and threw her on Corning, who had found his way to Wardley. Wardley climbed up in front of her, a new wound open on his leg.

From her position astride Corning, Dinah looked with horror at what her quest for a crown had brought. All around her were blood and bone and bodies, some piled waist high. Screams of pain and the stench of smoke mingled in the air.

Hell had come to Wonderland.

She had come to Wonderland.

Despite all this pain, her victory grew ever closer. Her Spades were at the gates now, cutting through dozens of Cards. Hundreds of her Yurkei were swarming and scaling the iron walls, as the few remaining archers sent arrows whizzing past their heads and shoulders.

"No, no, no." Wardley muttered as Dinah looked to see Xavier Juflee and his Heart Cards slaughter three Yurkei warriors with alarming ease. A trail of bodies lay behind him.

Juflee sensed that he was being watched and looked up, his eyes meeting theirs across the battlefield. Xavier curled his finger at Wardley, beckoning him to fight. Wardley shook his head. He would not fight his old mentor and friend.

A second trumpet blasted over the battlefield, its sound echoing across the valley. Every fighter turned to hear the words echoing down from the walls.

"Retreat! Retreat to inside the gates! The King of Hearts has ordered a retreat!"

There was a momentary pause as a quiet and refreshing wind blew around them. Then suddenly, all the Cards around Dinah ran for the iron gates, rushing through any Spades in their path, caring less about killing them and more about their own safety. The Cards pulled back, disappearing behind the protective iron swirls, but all for naught. It was done. She suspected the Cards had no idea that so many of her Yurkei fighters had made it over the wall. From behind the gates, she heard the intense rise of combat, followed by the quiet of surrender.

A few minutes later, the creak of ancient iron echoed out over the battlefield as the tall gates that protected the palace were thrown wide. With triumphant bellows, her remaining Yurkei and Spades flooded inside. Shouts of alarm rose up from inside the walls as hundreds of her men swarmed through the south gates. The push to open the gates to Mundoo's huge army on the north side had begun.

The area outside Wonderland Palace now held only small remnants of her army and the thousands of bodies that littered the ground. Xavier Juflee had disappeared. A few hundred Cards, somehow left behind in the retreat, placed their weapons on the ground and bowed before a bunch of furious Spades.

"Show them mercy!" Dinah screamed at them. "Or it will be *your* heads I take."

The Spades nodded obediently. Wardley turned Corning, and they galloped away from the palace, the bloodied white steed climbing swiftly up the hills. It was time for Dinah to regroup with the council and execute the rest of the plan.

She looked back over her shoulder at the palace. From there she could see it all: the fields of wildflowers now stained red, the pale horses of the Yurkei strewn lifelessly around the

palace, the vast stretch of death on the north side, where
Mundoo's army and the Cards continued to war against each
other. Dinah looked for Morte, but she could not see him
anywhere. He was gone—there was nothing she could do.
As Corning galloped away from the massacre, Dinah turned
her head to the turrets above the castle, where she prayed an
archer named Derwin Fergal was keeping his coat turned
the right way.

Q ♥

Seven

Dinah remembered the first time she had met Derwin Fergal: barely taller than his bow, even at twelve he had been rugged and stern, smiling curtly at Dinah before splitting an arrow to impress her. As a friend of Wardley's, Derwin would cross paths with Dinah occasionally at equestrian events where Wardley was competing, at croquet games, or at an endless parade of glittering balls that they both seemed to despise. Even then, Dinah could see that Derwin's focus was elsewhere, for even in the presence of a moody princess, his mind was solely on his arrows.

Upon turning sixteen, Derwin had entered the Heart Cards as a squire and worked his way up through the archer ranks until he served under Royan Eugedde, the lead archer. Derwin and Wardley grew apart as the Heart Cards pulled them in different directions, but they still remained friendly acquaintances. According to Wardley, there wasn't much that Derwin didn't already know about archery, so Eugedde stepped in as a father figure when Derwin's own father disappeared. Like so many others, he was swallowed into the folds of the Black Towers without so much as a warning. Derwin's talent grew as his anger about his father's imprisonment expanded. Rumor had it that he could kill a running deer from a thousand yards even through thick foliage, right through the neck, a clean shot. He sometimes boasted himself a better archer than most Yurkei, a wild claim to make even in Wonderland Palace.

Right before Dinah's world had collapsed in a sea of betrayal, Derwin had been named lead archer of the Heart Cards. His reputation was legendary, and so when Wardley suggested his name at one of Dinah's first war council meetings, Dinah and Cheshire had both sat forward with piqued interest. *A Fergal? On their side?*

The idea that a Fergal would fight for them was at first ludicrous, and yet now Dinah found herself putting her life—and the lives of those who meant the most to her—in the hands of that same boy who had tried to impress her so long ago.

"Do you think he can do it?" she whispered to Wardley.

He reached down and squeezed her hand. "If anyone can, it's him."

Corning continued to gallop up the hill outside the palace, with Dinah and Wardley sharing his back. Flecks of foamy blood poured out of his mouth. Wardley was whispering desperate words to his horse, almost unaware of Dinah's existence behind him. She tightened her arms around his waist, taking comfort in his touch, in the nearness of him. His hair smelled like it always had, of hay and lemons, but now he was covered with an unfamiliar stench—smoke and dried blood, the pungent odors making her eyes water. She closed them and, for just a second, let herself pretend that he was hers and they were riding together back to the palace, the kingdom, and nights in tangled sheets belonging to them alone.

Corning's steps slowed now as he made his way up that same hill where Dinah had watched the beginning of the battle unfold. Though it had been only a few hours, it seemed like a lifetime had passed. Dinah wasn't the same person she had once been, the same girl who had galloped down the hill full of battle rage, yearning for her fury to be satisfied. It wasn't. In fact, if she listened to her heart for just a moment, it seemed to be crying for more.

Dinah pushed the anger down, letting out a long breath as she surveyed the kingdom below.

"Are yeh ready?" Sir Gorrann was stepping up beside Corning, reaching for her hand. "Hurry, we don't have a lot of time."

Dinah kept her eyes on the turrets as she stepped backward, nearing the hastily built tent on the hill. Its purple fabric and Yurkei flags snapped in the wind as she ducked into the entrance. Inside, Cheshire was waiting for her, out of breath and bloodstained.

"Quickly! Get undressed," he snapped.

With Sir Gorrann's help, they stripped Dinah of her armor. First off was the breastplate, once white, now stained red, the broken heart spattered with mud. Cheshire worked his way down her legs, pulling off the black leather leg guards and the leather that was wrapped around her waist.

"What happened to your cape?"

Dinah shook her head. "Don't ask."

He grimaced. "Pity, I was quite fond of it."

The tent flap curled back and Dinah looked up as Wardley stomped in carrying a dusty bag. He looked battered, but more than that, he looked exhausted. Blood and brains were splashed across his sharp uniform. *He had killed so many. She had seen it.* Dinah reached around her wrist for the red ribbon hidden there and quickly tied her hair back.

"Do you have them?"

Wardley nodded and emptied the bag. The brown shapeless garments favored by the poor hit the floor with a thump. The smell of fish hit their noses hard.

"Are you sure this plan is necessary?" Dinah said sharply to Cheshire, who was loftily holding his nose.

"Not anymore," he answered with a shake of his head. "But I'll ponder the repercussions of this decision at a later time." He turned to Wardley as Dinah pulled the brown linen over her white tunic and black pants. The men in the tent followed suit.

"Is the Fergal boy on the south side?" Cheshire asked. Wardley was trying to scrub the blood off his cheeks with a rag, his face drawn.

Dinah answered for him. "Yes. He's there. I saw him."

When Morte had first ridden into battle, she had seen Derwin atop the turrets, his signature silver vest easy to spot as he fired arrow after arrow at the Yurkei from just inside the gates. Even with the white cranes' defensive maneuverings, he had managed to kill, at her count, probably fifty Yurkei and more than a few Spades. Dinah had watched both of Derwin's brothers get riddled with Yurkei arrows, and found herself wondering if he would stay the course, now that her army had killed his family. She watched him running up and down the turrets, a man most comfortable off the ground, a man who loved the whoosh of a shaft flying by his cheek. And now their fate was in his hands.

Dinah's breath pushed painfully out of her bruised lungs as she walked forward in her brown sack. At the back of the tent, a young Yurkei woman named Napayshi was being dressed in Dinah's armor—minus the breastplate. The Rebel Queen rested her hand against the girl's short black hair, unsure of how to feel and what to say.

"You don't have to do this," she muttered. "We can find another way."

"Damned hells she does," snapped Bah-kan, his entrance into the tent going unnoticed.

Napayshi took Dinah's hand in her own, running her smooth brown skin over Dinah's bloodstained palm. "It is my pleasure to die for my people, for Mundoo."

Her black eyes met Dinah's, and the look in them told Dinah that this woman's love for Mundoo was about more than just loyalty.

The woman leaned forward. "Do not mistake this as a gift for you. I will watch from the valley of the cranes as my people rise, watch as they take back their land. I will gladly die a weapon for the Yurkei." A small curl of blue smoke escaped from her lips.

Dinah bit down, trying not to inhale. *Damn the Caterpillar and Cheshire and their wicked, wicked plan.*

She remembered Cheshire's words as they had argued this plan, Dinah pleading against it until she could see no other way. *She is both a distraction and a weapon.*

Napayshi stood and squared her shoulders in the same way Dinah did. It felt strange watching this young thing become the fearful queen, the armor on her body blood-stained and dented. Blood that Dinah had drawn. Dents that Dinah had earned. The high collar of the armor shadowed the girl's face, and between the blood being splattered on her cheeks and her short black hair, even Dinah was impressed at how successful the transformation had been.

She turned to her motley group of supporters. "Let's get ready. We have to move quickly." Dinah, Cheshire, Wardley, Bah-kan, Ki-ershan, and Sir Gorrann all huddled together in their brown sacks.

"Ah, ah, ah." Cheshire reached down and plucked the

crown from her head with a chuckle. Dinah's hands flew to her hair. "You forgot this."

She felt naked without it, her hands absentmindedly tracing over her hair.

"You'll get it back," Cheshire hissed. "I swear on my life that a better crown than this will grace your head." Their eyes met.

Everyone was waiting for her, and so Dinah closed her eyes and drew a deep breath, once again steeling herself for battle. "The king waits for us."

All at once the two groups emerged from the tent, Napayshi out of the front, and a handful of brown-clothed paupers making their way out of the back. The fake queen climbed up on a black horse, tiny compared to the steed that Dinah had actually ridden. As Dinah watched, she felt a shard of pain twist in her heart. *Was Morte all right? Was he in pain somewhere, wondering where she was?* Even as she asked the questions, she knew that there was no way to answer them before this hellish day was over.

Dinah let her eyes rise up to the palace, past the pile of

bodies and the carrion-eaters that circled above them, the shadows of vultures already upon the forms of the dead, past the iron gates and past the walls to the turrets. A silver flash was moving now, up and down the stairs that linked various turrets and walkways at the front of the palace. Derwin.

Underneath the turrets, the Spades, once called traitors, now conquerors, were moving through the outskirts of the palace. Below Dinah, hordes of frightened women and children cried in the courtyard as they desperately clung to each other, searching for their fathers, their sons. Members of the court were taking up arms, standing in front of their homes that lay just outside the main palace walls. Dinah barely glanced at them. She could not linger on what would happen to them, not now. She could only save them one way, by getting into the palace without killing thousands more on the way in.

She watched as Derwin rounded the south side of the castle and got into position. He raced across the stables and above the towering iron gates, which were now swarming with Yurkei. Without stopping, Derwin sent arrows into the skulls of two invaders who tried to stop him. Dinah closed her eyes. *I'm sorry, I'm sorry, but he has a part to play.* Her men screamed as they fell to their deaths, *her men*. The line of betrayal was so fine in war, it was practically made of sand.

Dinah watched carefully now as Derwin took a wide stance, two fellow archers slumped over the wall beside him. She took a deep breath and looked away as Derwin took aim. There were shouts from all around her as the Spades sprinted toward their fake queen, sitting on her horse far from anyone's reach on the hill outside the palace. The remaining Yurkei were running too, their wild screams attracting the attention of the cluster of Heart Cards on the south side of the palace. From underneath her crusted brown hood, Dinah watched as Derwin Fergal loaded his longbow with a specially designed arrow, one created for speed and distance—and looked over the tower to the Rebel Queen's army. The Heart Cards were moving slowly toward the Yurkei girl now, their eyes on Derwin, praying and hoping that this boy would do what no one else could. The archer stopped moving. Dinah looked back at Napayshi, sitting there atop her black steed, the crown of red upon her head, regal, beautiful, and a symbol of her people. Ready to die. The fake queen was yelling orders at the men in a good impression of Dinah's proud and haughty voice as she started galloping closer to the palace, drawing the Cards near her. Dinah exhaled and let all the air rush out of her lungs. One shot.

Sir Gorrann and Wardley stepped in front of Dinah, just in case, always protective of their queen. Dinah raised herself up on the tips of her toes to see over their shoulders, letting everything fall away from her—the battle, the palace, the king—and let her vision tunnel onto only the Yurkei woman. There was only Derwin and the girl everyone thought was the queen. He aimed the arrow right at her beating heart. Dinah stopped for a moment to look at the palace, black hair falling across her cheeks. *He could not fail.*

Derwin released his arrow. It darted past his cheek, flying straight and true. It sailed steadily past the palace walls, unyielding as a hawk as it barreled down upon the Yurkei girl. The arrow struck with such force that it propelled her backward off the horse and onto the ground. She let out a loud scream as her body was punched into the ground, the terrible sound echoing in Dinah's ears, a memory she knew was marring her heart like a scar. She grimaced as the world went silent. The red glass heart shimmered in the light from where it pierced her chest. The girl sat propped up like a rag doll, the arrow stuck far out of her back, a blossom of dark blood seeping from her chest. Napayshi was dead before she hit the ground.

Dinah felt like she was going to be sick. Wardley swallowed beside her, his face pale. "Well, that was about as horrible as I thought it was going to be."

Dinah pushed back her bile. "No. It was worse."

Joyful screams rang out below. The Heart Cards guarding the south side of the palace sprinted toward Napayshi's body. Cards everywhere were shouting in glee, dropping their weapons, hugging each other.

"The Rebel Queen is dead!"

Dinah was shoved forward as a crowd surged and gathered around the body.

"It's the queen! The Rebel Queen!" shouted Wardley, his voice disguised. "She's dead! The war is won!"

Dinah, Cheshire, Wardley, Ki-ershan, Sir Gorrann, and Bah-kan picked up the girl's body and began carrying it on their shoulders toward the palace. Dinah felt the girl's weight roll across her back, and red blood dripped from the girl's chest onto Dinah's cheek, making its way slowly down her face. Napayshi's blood was still warm. The Heart Cards clustered around her.

"Is it the queen? Is she dead?"

Sir Gorrann's voice was clipped. "Yes, sirs, I did see this queen felled by an arrow only a moment ago."

"Yes, we all saw it," snapped one, a higher-ranking Heart Card whose name escaped Dinah.

"Why are you touching her, you filthy maggots? This body needs to be brought to the king, immediately."

Dinah and her men put the body down carefully, her heart thudding so loud that she swore the Cards could hear it. One wrong move, and these men would kill her whole party.

"Bring her inside the gates, quickly!"

The Heart Cards grabbed Napayshi's corpse and hauled it away from the false peasants, heading toward the palace.

Dinah and her men stepped back before weaving away from the Heart Cards, making their way to the south side of the palace. On the hill, the pounding of drums rang out over the battlefield, and the wailing of both Yurkei and Spade filled the air. Dinah ducked as a flurry of arrows began showering around the Heart Cards as they ran with the body past the gate and into the courtyard, on their way to the king.

Dinah could see inside the palace walls as Napayshi's body began to jerk and spasm, reacting to the massive amounts of blue smoke that were about to be released. As her blood cooled, the liquid form of the Caterpillar's drug of choice would hit the air and vaporize.

"What the hells? What is that?"

It was starting.

She heard alarmed shouts from behind her as both Heart Cards and villagers grew confused. Blue smoke began vaporizing out of the dead queen's nose and mouth. The Heart Cards were bent over and coughing as the blue smoke entered their lungs. She knew from experience that soon they would pass into a pleasant haze, unaware of what was happening.

As she watched, the courtyard below quickly filled with the hazy blue smoke that now poured from Napayshi's body in great waves. Chaos ensued as people scrambled to get away from the sneaking tendrils; but they were too late. Dinah watched with growing happiness as the stampeding peasants and Cards slowed. They stopped yelling, stopped moving. Contented smiles crept across their faces, and they started murmuring happily to themselves. In minutes, an angry horde of citizens and Cards ready to defend their palace was turned into a courtyard full of simpletons, happy hallucinations playing out in front of their eyes.

With the drug, Dinah's army had neutralized the violence on her side of the palace and distracted the Heart Cards. Now their job was to get to the king, who would be in the keep.

"Quit dallying," muttered Sir Gorrann. "She's dead. Let's go."

Dinah's party ran for the small clump of wildflowers about half a mile outside the main wall, with another group of Spades following far behind. Dinah looked up onto the turrets and saw a fleeting flash of silver as Derwin climbed down from the turrets. She saluted briefly, and an arrow hit the ground beside her with a thump, an acknowledgment that Derwin Fergal had done his duty. His name would grace the lips of his children's children, and he would forever be etched into the history books as either the man who killed the Rebel Queen or the man who helped a queen stage a coup. Either way, Derwin Fergal would come out on top.

Dinah and her men reached the mossy grass and the clump of flowers that circled it. "I know it's here, I know it's here." Dinah was frantically searching the ground, shoving dirt aside, ripping up weeds that hadn't been trimmed for years.

Bah-kan stepped forward. "Are you sure this is the spot? I remember seeing a map of the palace that had the secret entrances—"

"Shut up!" barked Dinah. "Shut up. Everyone."

No one said a word. Dinah stood up, turned around, and looked at the sun, remembering the thin slat of moonlight that had led her out that night, the night that she had met Vittiore for the first time, when Cheshire had shown her the tunnels. The moonlight that had come from . . .

there. She stepped over about ten feet and squatted. Within seconds her fingers had found the grooves in the earth and traced the line of the trapdoor in the dirt.

She flung it open and grinned at her men as a cloud of rotted dust settled over her. She winked at Cheshire in a rare moment of good humor, and he handed her a torch.

Dinah cleared her throat. "I believe our revenge awaits. Now, on your knees, men."

Below her, the secret passageways into the palace were as empty and still as they had been that night so many years ago.

Eight

Darkness consumed Dinah. She was far underneath the earth, the smell of wet dirt overcoming her senses. For a moment she was desperately alone, clawing at the mud around her. Finally, she waved the flame of her pink torch past her face, where the flaring light illuminated her harsh features.

"Are you sure it's this way?" hissed Wardley, two steps behind her. "I think we're lost."

"Trust me." Dinah waved the torch again. The tunnel should be here—she knew it. But . . . aha! She crouched down and crawled through a small hole in the earth, pushing her way through a thin layer of dirt that had filled the tunnel since she had last been here. Worms and spiders and *gods knew what else* fell around her as she pushed through the dirt. The black roots twisted above her head, and Dinah could hear the roots reaching for her, seeking to envelop her familiar mind and body.

With a cry, she pushed through the opening. Wardley's hand wrapped around her ankle. A thin wall of dirt collapsed under her outstretched hand, and Dinah pushed herself through the showering muck. Her head emerged in a wide tunnel, long forgotten and freezing. *Yes, yes, this was right.* Through the darkness, Dinah could see the thin tunnel stretched out in front of her.

"We're in," she whispered. She pushed herself up to her feet and waited for the others to emerge from the small space. Wardley, Ki-ershan, Sir Gorrann, Bah-kan, Cheshire, and a dozen of their strongest Spades picked their way through the tunnels behind her. Dinah held her torch high, her eyes taking in her surroundings. It was all familiar now, the biting cold of the tunnels, the damp earth, the black roots. Dinah ran forward, her hands touching the walls.

"Yes, yes, I think we go through here!"

"Dinah, stop!" ordered Wardley. "Wait for us!"

Dinah paused and took a few deep breaths, waiting for Wardley to catch up. The quiet moment wrenched open her memory of the battle: Morte crashing into the waves of Heart Cards. Her sword sinking into a neck, a stomach. Yur-Jee's throat slit wide. Such terrible things, and yet the feeling inside her wasn't one of despair. Dinah gave herself a shake. *Focus. Focus.* After a few seconds, Wardley emerged next to her. They were both bloodied and worn from the toll of battle.

"Are you all right?"

Dinah tried to ignore how near he was to her. His scent, his comfort, the heat of his skin—it was enough to drive her mad, and the last thing she needed to feel right now was distraction and despair. She brushed him off.

"I'm so close," she murmured to him softly, "so close now to the man who killed Charles and stole my crown. I can't lose my head down here, but—Wardley. The battle. So much blood."

What she didn't share with the boy she loved was that the black fury was churning inside her now, alive and starving, and Dinah was prepared to feed it to her heart's content. Everything she touched seemed to tingle with life. She was awake, and her sword longed for vengeance.

Sir Gorrann appeared through the small hole in the ground, the pink flames of his torch dancing over his weathered face. "Yer telling me that this really is the easiest way into the palace? Yeh made it sound like a stroll across the croquet court." He gave Dinah a smile that she was unable to return.

Cheshire edged up beside them, his normally pristine face and hair smudged with dirt. She barely recognized him without his usual adornments and purple cloak. "Yes, she's right, it's through here." He nodded. "I'm almost certain this tunnel leads out to the tapestry near the king's privy, which will take us out into the Great Hall."

"And where exactly will the king be?" thundered Bahkan, who could not keep quiet no matter how much they shushed him. He clutched his Heartsword close to his chest, his forearms stained with the blood of dead Cards.

"The king will be in the keep, which is above the Great Hall," answered Cheshire. "He will be there with his council, and Queen Vittiore."

"She is not a queen," answered Dinah icily. "She is a stranger upon the throne."

"And an innocent," Wardley reminded her firmly. "Someone who the king used, just like you. We need her to get the people on your side."

Dinah took a deep breath. "I know."

A painful groan escaped Sir Gorrann's lips as he braced himself against a wall. He had a wound in his thigh leaking blood and a gash across his shoulder, but wouldn't let anyone come close enough to tend either. The Spade was obviously exhausted. After a moment's respite, he continued down the tunnels. "Come. Let's finish this. When this palace finds out you're alive, the armies will continue to tear each other apart. Yeh need the majority of the people within these walls to live. Iu-Hora's smoke lasts less than two hours. The Yurkei won't wait forever to raid the city, and the King of Hearts won't hold back his worst. They will both unleash their rage, until there is no one left to fight their war except the children."

"Then let's stop talking about it and make haste," agreed Dinah. "Follow me." She began running through the tunnels, weaving through doorways and up muddy stone steps without thinking. Something inside her was sure these were the steps she had taken three times before. She knew these tunnels, and it seemed the more she thought about it, the more lost she became.

"Yes," whispered Cheshire, who had slithered up beside her. "I remember now, this is the way. Follow us!" he bellowed backward.

"Will the king be waiting for us?" she whispered to him, her breaths coming quick and heavy.

"Without a doubt," he answered grimly. "But he has no idea that we are coming up *through* the castle. Right now he thinks we are still outside the gates. He also thinks that you are dead, which means the element of surprise will work highly in our favor. His plan was to wait us out—the fool thinks we mean to lay siege to the palace. Trust me, my dear, the king, at this very moment, has let his guard down. Trust in your decoy. She was very convincing." He gave a sinister smile.

Dinah still didn't feel right about Napayshi, who was now nothing more than a pile of flesh pouring blue smoke. She shivered.

"We're almost there," she announced to her men. "Draw your weapons."

Sir Gorrann walked through their ranks. "Keep them close to your body, inside your cloaks."

Dinah could hear the unsheathing of metal and iron. She clasped her sword close to her heart. They had reached a thick wooden door. Covering the door was a woven tapestry that she knew featured her father, mounted on Morte, his Heartsword drawn, looking like the most fearsome warrior the kingdom had ever known. *And she was going to kill him.*

Beyond the tapestry lay the Great Hall, no doubt filled with Wonderland citizens, women and children who were gathered in a safe refuge from the fighting.

"Remember who we are, and who we are not," Wardley intoned to the men. He wrapped his hand roughly around

Dinah's arm. "Especially you. Don't lose your head. You might not be his blood heir, but you share his impulsiveness."

Annoyed, Dinah shook off his grip and pushed the door open, flinging the tapestry aside. They were in a narrow hallway that led out behind the throne. The group emerged from the tunnels disguised in their ragged cloaks, rope belts cinched around their waists. Hopefully, the hordes of people in the Great Hall would think that they were simply peasants taking refuge in a place they didn't belong. Who could care about such things while the enemy broke down their walls?

"Are we ready?" asked Dinah.

Sir Gorrann pushed past her. "I'll go first." Ki-ershan stood in front of Dinah, every sculpted muscle in his body poised and ready to attack. Sir Gorrann stepped around the tapestry, stepping out into the Great Hall. Dinah followed behind him, her head down.

She paused, her mouth open in shock. Wardley pushed past her, a look of disgust upon his face. "How could . . . ?" He stopped. "Where are they?"

The Great Hall was empty. The room, so vast and

grand, was a thousand times larger than Dinah remembered. Here was the gold throne, with its etched hearts. Here was the heart window, bathing the room in red light, and there was the box above the hall, where she and Wardley met to share secrets. Dinah was home again, but there was no one here, not a single person.

"Where are the townspeople?" Even Cheshire looked bewildered.

"They're in the streets," answered Sir Gorrann. "They were sent outside."

Wardley gritted his teeth and clutched his sword. "What the hell kind of king does not offer the protection of his palace to his people in a time of war?"

I've had enough. Dinah pulled her brown cloak off. Her hair shimmered in the red light, making it appear as if her head was made of flame.

She drew her sword. "The kind of king who's going to die today."

Sir Gorrann let out a gasp. "Why are you taking off your cloak? Stop!"

Dinah turned on him, her eyes filled with a righteous

rage. "I left this palace, my home, covered in a cloak, running for my life, a scared child. I will not return as a peasant in disguise, as a fearful girl. I return as a queen, as a woman, here to claim her rightful throne. Come on, let's find him, now!"

The inspired men around her let out a cheer and they all ran toward the door, weapons drawn, cloaks left behind. Bah-kan flung open the doors to the Great Hall. Two Heart Cards were stationed outside the empty hall, and Dinah actually pitied them as they watched the enemy emerge from the doors behind them. Bah-kan dispatched them quickly and brutally. The group ran through the empty marble hallways. Ladies and lords, servants and children opened their doors at the sound of footsteps. When they saw the group, they pulled back into their living quarters, terrified.

"Get back!" Dinah screamed at the idiots as they passed. "Shut and lock your doors!" Her directions were followed without question.

Together, her band of fighters raced up the stone staircases that led to the keep, one after another, until it felt like they could climb no more. Finally, they emerged into a wide room, where a collection of weapons was assembled under Wonderland's most priceless art. In the corner of the dark hall was a single spiral staircase that led up to the keep.

Her group came to a jagged halt. At the base of the stairway, two dozen Heart Cards stood in a silent line, assembled like an elaborate chessboard, their red-and-white uniforms decked with pins and medals. At the front stood Xavier Juflee, the commander of the Heart Cards, his shield clasped against one breast, a sword in his other hand. As Dinah's fighters filled the room, the Heart Cards drew their weapons. There was a moment of stillness as both parties surveyed the scene and anticipated the coming violence.

Juflee's eyes widened when he saw Dinah.

"What the hells?" he gasped. "I saw you die."

Several of the Heart Cards stepped backward in awe.

Dinah stepped forward and addressed Xavier in a low voice. "Xavier. We do not come seeking violence. I come seeking my rightful throne from your king. If you step aside, each of you will be granted mercy and maintain your current position. For your own sake, surrender. Otherwise there will be much bloodshed here. Please, I'm begging you."

Xavier took a moment to regain his composure, his surprise at her appearance fading away before he smiled meanly at her. "I cannot do that, Princess. You return here a murderer and a traitor, and I'll take pleasure in mounting your head for the king. That is, unless *you* surrender."

Dinah gave a sad shake of her head. She stepped backward into the protective folds of her men. Xavier raised his arm, and Dinah did the same. She let out a shout, and her fighters rushed past her, the groups melding together in seconds. The tiny room filled with the sounds of swords and screams. The two sides battled, Dinah aiding where she could. She would not be injured now, not while she was so close to the king.

The battle raged for several minutes, until Xavier Juflee cut through his rapidly diminishing line and rushed toward her, his sword arcing through the air near her throat. In a flash, Wardley's sword sliced in front of her and then Xavier and Wardley were dancing, their swords clinging together. They spun and leaped, moving faster than she had ever seen either of them move. Wardley kept trying to step back from the fight as Xavier engaged him, again and again. Finally, Xavier became frustrated, spitting and cursing at Wardley.

"Why won't you fight me, boy?"

Wardley pushed him back before landing an ugly scratch across Xavier's cheek. "Because you were my friend and I don't want to kill you!" he screamed. "I don't. But if you come near her again, I will!"

Xavier laughed. "You couldn't."

A deep growl penetrated the room as Bah-kan strolled forward.

"I could, and I will!"

Without warning, Bah-kan launched himself at Xavier with terrifying speed. The entire room seemed to pause as Bah-kan's and Xavier Juflee's swords clanged together, a sound so loud that Dinah felt it in her chest. Bah-kan brought his massive sword sweeping down toward Xavier, who narrowly avoided its blade by leaping and bouncing off the wall. With his momentum propelling him, Xavier pushed Bah-kan forward and brought his heart-studded blade against his opponent's throat. Bah-kan answered by flinging Xavier against a wall and bringing his own blade down, just missing Xavier's head. Xavier moved to the side just in time, and Bah-kan's sword buried itself in the wall. With a roar, he quickly yanked it out, sending a shower of tiny pebbles over them both. Again and again, their swords met and released, and Dinah felt dizzy watching them, both so skilled, the best fighters she had ever seen, circling each other like lions.

The fighting continued around her. Ki-ershan bested the Heart's second-in-command with a quick slice to the belly, while one of the Cards killed three of Dinah's best Spades. Wardley stepped backward and easily dispatched a sneaky Heart Card who was quietly moving toward Dinah.

She smelled the blood all around her. Outside, there had been the sky and the soil, things to ground her in the fight. Here, in this tiny space, the reality of battle was so much more suffocating, so much more potent.

Wardley severed the arm of a Heart Card before plunging his sword into the dying man's stomach. Cheshire's daggers found a few necks, the men staring down bewildered and confused before falling face-first onto the floor. Sir Gorrann battled with two Cards and succeeded in knocking them against each other, his blade plunging through both of their shoulders. They fell to the ground with whimpered cries for mercy. It turned out even the highest Cards could be brought low by war. Sir Gorrann, panting with effort, raised his sword above their heads before looking at Dinah.

Dinah shook her head. "Give them the mercy they ask for," she commanded. Sir Gorrann stepped back. She watched as her men quickly gained the advantage and dispatched the rest of the king's guards. Many were given mercy—and some were not.

Soon only Xavier and Bah-kan remained fighting, both spattering blood on the slick stone floor. Xavier's head wound was bleeding; Bah-kan was oozing blood from a gash at his side. Weariness had overtaken them and their strokes became slower and more desperate. Even the wounded Cards watched in awe, each man aware that this was the best duel they would ever witness.

Xavier looked into Bah-kan's face. "I know you," he hissed. "Stern Ravier, once a notorious Club but now a traitor and a Yurkei, all dressed up in feathers. Tell me, do you have little traitors at home, with some whore Yurkei wife?"

Bah-kan landed a blow to the Knave of Hearts with the blunt pommel of his sword, knocking the man backward. Xavier's shield scuttled across the room.

Bah-kan shook his sword and roared. "I was born a Club, but I will die a Yurkei, full of honor and glory. And when I die, I will rise up with the cranes and shit on your grave!"

Xavier leaped forward again, his sword raised overhead. Dinah saw the opportunity that had presented itself. Bah-kan, moving quickly now, brought the sword up through the man's ribs. It exploded out of his back and the Knave of Hearts slumped forward onto the blade. Bah-kan stepped back and roared, his attention diverted to his own pleasure a moment too soon. Xavier, a loyal Card unto his death, saw his moment and with his last burst of energy plunged his sword through Bah-kan's neck. They both fell to the ground, entangled in death, their blood mixing on the ground.

"Bah-kan! No, no!" Dinah gave a scream of agony as she pushed Xavier's body aside and cradled Bah-kan's massive head in her hands. His eyes looked up at her in alarm and disbelief. "Oh, Bah-kan, I'm so sorry. I'm so sorry."

She gently kissed his forehead. His eyes blinked rapidly as he smiled up at her through the blood, which was all over him, and all over her. He was heavy in her arms, her great warrior, the great Club, a man who had lived—and died—twice.

"My queen," he mouthed, his throat gurgling. He began speaking rapid Yurkei words. His eyes blinked once before they looked blankly up at the ceiling, his chest rising no more. Dinah bent her head over his, her cheek resting on his still face. There was silence in the hall, even from the Cards whose lives had been spared. Tears dripped off her chin, smearing the white paint that covered Bah-kan's face. She wiped them away.

"He will have a warrior's funeral. We'll bury him in Hu-Yuhar, his true home." She turned to the Cards who lay wounded near Sir Gorrann's feet. She kicked one in the side, and he grunted in pain before she curled her fingers around his chin. Her black eyes bore into his. "You will keep this body safe and unblemished, do you understand me? If anything happens to him, I will come for you, and my mercy will be just a memory."

The two men stared up at Dinah, their faces full of terror. They nodded. "Yes, my queen."

Nine

Dinah took a deep breath, tearing her eyes away from Bahkan's still form to look at the men who surrounded her: Cheshire, Wardley, Sir Gorrann, Ki-ershan. Her eyes met Sir Gorrann's. They mirrored hers at the moment: the hunger for vengeance, the promise of it so close at last. She was weary with grief, and her hands shook from emotion and exhaustion. She knew what must be done, what must be said. It filled her with fear, but the anger inside her held down her doubts, the taste of it like metal between her teeth. She turned to the men.

"I alone will fight the king. I will not have anyone else die for me today. It must be me. Otherwise I could lose my claim to the throne. Do you understand?"

Wardley stepped forward and grabbed her roughly, his hands squeezing her shoulder blades together. "Dinah, I will not let him kill you."

"People will not respect a leader who sends others to do her bidding. Isn't this why I fought in the battle in the first place? I will show all those people in there"—she pointed her sword toward the door—"that I am not afraid of a king who has worn out his rule."

"Dinah . . ." Wardley's eyes filled with tears. "I can't lose you today. Not now. We've come so far."

She gave him a small smile and reached up to trace his cheek. "Wardley . . ." Her fingers left his face to touch the bare spot upon her head where her crown normally sat. "Obey me."

Wardley dropped his head, hands clenched at his sides.

Dinah walked forward and entered the keep, her men following behind.

Inside the fortified towers above the Great Hall was a

sparsely decorated room, stocked for a siege. Crates of food and weapons leaned against the walls, which were lined with Heart Cards and dozens of men from noble houses. The king's council stood around a raised platform that held a makeshift throne. Atop it sat the King of Hearts. He had aged greatly in the year since Dinah had seen him. His shoulder-length blond hair was streaked with patchy gray. The king's massive body, once stout and sturdy, had grown soft and portly. His arms remained huge and veiny, though, and Dinah could see muscles bulging beneath his armor. His face was blotchy and red, his blue eyes bloodshot and narrowed.

The King of Hearts clutched his Heartsword against his chest and barely raised his chin when Dinah and her men came through the door. She immediately understood that this was part of a performance, in which she had a starring role. He would not stand for her presence, a sign that she wasn't the queen in his eyes. To him, she was no more than a commoner. The crowd parted silently as Dinah stepped toward the platform.

The king gave her a condescending smile. "I thought I

heard my wicked daughter's voice. And here I thought you were dead. Instead I see you've come to steal my crown, you ungrateful wretch."

Dinah forced herself to look straight into his face, though her legs gave a shake underneath her. The King of Hearts—her father, or so she had believed—could always scare her, destroy her. Not today. Today she would not let him pull her apart from the inside out and turn every good thing to dust. Dinah struggled to keep her confidence, her heart pounding so loudly she feared the entire room could hear.

"Not steal. I've come to claim the throne that is mine by birth. My mother was Queen Davianna, and so the crown should rightfully pass to me instead of Vittiore, who has no claim on the throne. I come here to repair the land that you have broken, to reap justice for all the innocents that you have murdered or imprisoned, and to free the Yurkei people from your greedy oppression."

Fury passed over the king's face and he stood, his Heartsword glinting in the late-afternoon light. His voice rose to a roar. "You shall not speak treason to me in my own palace! You weak, pathetic girl. From the moment you were born, you disgusted me, with your cries and your neediness. You are not my daughter, I know it in my bones. *You*, with your black hair, are your mother's bastard child! Proof that she was as much of a whore as I suspected! No child of mine would turn against me."

"No?" screamed Dinah, losing control quickly. "What about your son? Did he turn against you? Charles was your son! He was innocent!"

The king erupted in anger, a vein throbbing in his forehead. "You will not speak his name, you murderous bitch!" He motioned to the Heart Cards. "Kill them all. Each one. Off with their heads!"

The Cards took a hesitant step toward Dinah's men. Sir Gorrann raised his sword just as a terrible sound tore through the room, causing everyone to pause. Everyone turned toward the windows of the keep as the horrific reverberation of iron bending filled the room. Walls shook as heavy stones crashed to the ground. Dinah's army had opened the gates on the north side. From the courtyard below came the terrified screams of women and children, followed by the loud whooping of the Yurkei and the thundering of hooves. Mundoo's large Yurkei army was now flooding inside the walls.

At the sound of the gates falling, the king's face went pale. He had lost. Dinah's mind raced; she needed to address the people, and quickly, or it would all descend into chaos and even more violence. She lowered her voice as she stared at the king.

"It's over. Our armies have broken down your walls. In an hour's time we will take all of Wonderland Palace. I beg of you, surrender and save the men who defend you here. Their lives are still worth something to me."

"You speak like a queen," answered the king. "But you will die a traitor, a worthless wench, a motherless orphan, a murderer, a girl I never wished to call daughter."

"That's because she isn't your daughter."

Cheshire stepped forward.

The king's face burned as he looked at Cheshire, his most trusted adviser and companion. "You!"

Cheshire brushed off the king's anger as if it were nothing more than a drop of rain. The king pointed at him.

"You treacherous, slimy leech. Your speech is poison to

any who hear it! You served me loyally for almost twenty years and then you desert me for her? For this simpering creature?" The king began laughing hysterically. "I'll wipe off her blood from my Heartsword on your ribs."

Cheshire laughed casually. "Are you so dim that you never suspected she was *my* daughter? Can't you see her? The dark hair, the dark eyes, her sharp mind. She certainly didn't get that from you. Davianna never loved you. Tell me, did she even have reason to try? You, with your whores and your pointless wars, you never gave her a minute of your day." A shadow crossed over Cheshire's face, and his pointed smile turned angry. "I loved her. Physically and mentally, *she was mine*. She was always mine. I watched as you killed her from neglect and abuse. Had you embraced our daughter, there wouldn't be an army breaking down your walls. But you couldn't, because you are a prideful, lustful man who needs to possess everything he sees. You are not the ruler these people deserve, but Dinah is. She is the queen they will love for a hundred years, and as our family rises, your name will be wiped from this kingdom like dust from a mirror."

There came a roaring sound, and Dinah realized a

great horde was coming up the stairs behind them. Were they trapped, caught between two enemies? She turned as dozens of Yurkei swarmed up through the doors of the keep. A handful of wooden arrows flew into the room and buried themselves in the exposed necks of a few Heart Cards. They fell face-first onto the floor.

"Stop!" shouted Dinah. The Yurkei at the top of the stairs hesitated.

"Surrender," Dinah shouted at the king, aware that she longed greatly for the lives of everyone gathered in the room to be spared. She spread her hands. "Please gods, surrender! What are you doing?"

The king gave her a raw smile and curled his finger toward her. Dinah paused, unsure what to do. Then, like a coiled snake, he leaped at her, his Heartsword ripping through the air. Dinah leaned back just in time, and the blade of the sword cut deep into her chin. She felt the warm trickle of blood down her neck. *It's happening*, she thought.

She had time to think no more. Her sword rose up and met his Heartsword in midair. The sharp, piercing clang seemed to freeze everyone in the room. Again and again their swords met, his Heartsword flashing so rapidly that Dinah quickly focused only on meeting his blows, not getting in any of her own. He nicked the upper part of her arm, twice. She winced as her blood spattered on the floor around her.

The king raised his sword and smiled. "I might take you piece by piece, little girl."

Dinah held her sword steady and thought of Bah-kan, of the things he had taught her, of the things that Sir Gorrann and Wardley had taught her. Taking a deep breath, she let her mind swirl like a furious wind, ripping through every piece of knowledge that she had. She swiped wide and missed. She swung again and her blade skimmed past his neck, pulling her off balance. The King of Hearts, seeing his opportunity, reached out and grabbed Dinah's hair, bringing his Heartsword up to meet her neck. As Dinah spun herself away from his grip, she managed to swing one of her legs around in a forceful kick, hitting his chest with all her strength. The king fell back a few feet, surprised and gasping for air. It was enough. She advanced and swung her sword at his heart, catching him hard on the ribs.

In her haste, Dinah had swung with more force than necessary, and her sword bounced off his armor and skittered across the floor. She crawled after it, narrowly avoiding the wide, swinging arcs made by the enraged king. His Heartsword landed blows on either side of her, one after another, as she bobbed and weaved on the floor. Wardley, his face terrified and furious, kicked her sword toward her. Dinah grabbed the blade and raised it above her head.

The king was everywhere around her now, swinging relentlessly, leaving Dinah barely able to protect herself. But his unnecessarily large strokes left him vulnerable. Dinah was able to plow her foot into his leg, smashing part of his knee with her heavy boot. He howled in pain, giving Dinah enough time to get up off the floor. His eyes met hers as he stood up, limping now, more furious than ever. They were both breathing heavily, and those around them watched in awed silence.

Dinah was aware, from a spring deep in her mind, that she was outmatched by the king. He was a better fighter, a better swordsman. She had hoped that the years of drinking and womanizing had slowed his arm, but they had not.

Realistically, she had no prayer of beating him, only holding him off until she was too exhausted to fight any longer. This was what Wardley had been trying to tell her. She would not win.

The king was advancing on her now, rapidly, in spite of his injured leg. Her long blade matched his Heartsword in the air, in front of her, behind her. They spun and danced, moving faster and faster as they both became more desperate to end the fight. The blows were coming closer to her chest now, and her clothing was marked with the long gouges that spoke of the Heartsword's fondness for slashing.

She'd survived the wilds of Wonderland, raised an army, and returned to her home, but she would be defeated here, her life snuffed out by the very man who had taken everything else from her. *It was so desperately unfair.* In her mind she cried out to the silent Wonderland gods—could there be a worse fate? Dinah leaned on the edge of her sword, just for a moment, to catch the breath that she so desperately needed. The King of Hearts grinned and wiped a smear of blood from his cheek.

"Are you ready to die, Princess? I daresay, it's long

overdue. I should have killed you the moment you emerged from your mother's womb. Maybe it's time you went to meet her."

Dinah's arms trembled as she raised her sword for what she knew would be the last round. She was so tired, more exhausted than she had ever been in her life. Even death would be a relief from this effort, and if so, she would meet it boldly, hurtling toward the darkness. She would not let him take her gently. Her legs shook beneath her, her entire body screamed with the effort. The king clutched his Heartsword and stepped back, preparing to launch his final wave of attack.

Sir Gorrann stepped forward from the crowd and looked at the king, shaking his head. "Amabel. Ioney," he said softly. "Amabel and Ioney." He began repeating their names, louder and louder. "Amabel. Ioney."

"What are you raving about, you treacherous Spade?" screamed the king. "Shut your mouth or I'll cut out your tongue when I'm done with her!"

Sir Gorrann stayed still, but the names grew louder. "Amabel, Ioney."

Wardley understood instantly and joined in. "Amabel, Ioney, Faina Baker, Bah-kan."

Cheshire raised his voice. "Davianna."

Together they repeated the names. "Amabel, Ioney, Faina Baker, Bah-kan, Davianna . . ."

The Spades around the room began to chime in with their own names, names that Dinah had never heard. And the Yurkei followed behind them, the names of their fallen like music, rising through the room. The voices grew louder, a cacophony of sound that filled the space. The remaining Cards in the room eyed each other with caution, until one brave Heart Card stepped toward Dinah, his head bowed.

"Eliza Grotton. Forsham Smith."

He dropped his sword on the ground and bent his knee. After a moment, other Cards followed him. The room was filled now with a chorus of names, growing louder with each brave soul who voiced them, the names of loved ones murdered, imprisoned, missing . . . all under the rule of the King of Hearts.

Sir Gorrann stepped closer to the king. "Amabel, Ioney." He raised his eyebrow at Dinah. Dinah looked up at the king. Everything now seemed to move slowly, as if each movement was underwater.

"I am the king!" he screamed back at them, and with a roar, he swung his Heartsword at Dinah's bare neck. She threw herself forward and fell toward the floor, his blade catching the edge of her ear before digging sharply into the side of her head. White-hot pain ricocheted past her eyeballs, and without thinking, she clutched her open hand to the wound.

Blood poured from the gash, spilling over her forehead and nose. The king hesitated for a moment to look down with contempt at his weak daughter, frantically wiping the blood from her eyes so that she might see.

"You foolish child."

He raised his arm. It was the moment Dinah needed, the one she had planned for. She saw the opening in his armor, a tiny notch just above his heart where the metal curled up and away from his chest. With every last ounce of strength in her body, Dinah leaped up, ducking past the blade that swung for her throat. Leaving herself wide open, she plunged her sword through the space in his armor and then pushed as deeply as she could. She felt his muscle separate, felt the throbbing rhythm vibrate up her sword as it tore through his beating heart.

The king's blue eyes went wide with shock. He stumbled once, and again, with Dinah's sword held aloft by his body, like a gruesome marionette. A line of blood appeared at the corner of his mouth, and he looked with surprise at the people gathered around him.

"Not," he muttered, "not by her."

Dinah pushed him down, the crown falling roughly from his head as he was forced to kneel in front of her. She looked into his pale and sweaty face, his mouth open and closing like a dying fish. A guttural rattle escaped his lips as her black eyes bore into his slack face. Her hand twisted around the sword handle, and she pulled the blade from his heart. The king slumped forward against her, his mouth opened in silent pain. One last time, Dinah looked upon his face. This sad man, her father, her king—was no longer either.

"Charles," she whispered in his ear. "For Charles."

His face turned to her, his features nearly motionless as

he fought to keep death at bay. His blue eyes found hers, and the last emotion to pass through them was not hatred, but confusion. "Charles?" His last breath washed over her face, warm and sour.

Dinah gently laid him down on the floor, his head near his makeshift throne. The king was dead.

"I am the queen," she breathed quietly, before wrapping her fingers tightly around his crown.

Q
♥

Ten

There was silence in the keep as Dinah stared out at the Cards. Dizzy from blood loss, she felt the room spin.

"Drop your weapons!" she ordered her men. The Yurkei lowered their bows and the Spades gingerly placed their swords on the ground. She turned to the men who had sworn to protect their king, holding the flesh wound on her head with one trembling hand.

"I do not long for your lives, and you are not my prisoners. You are the Cards of Wonderland Palace, and I hope to have you in my service. I would ask that you stay here in the keep until I can return. Then we may discuss the terms of your service, not with chains and swords, but with pen and paper. Do you find this agreeable?"

The bold Card who had spoken the names of the deceased to the king stepped forward. "I speak for these Cards and lords, Your Majesty. We will do as you ask, if you spare the lives of our families."

"Of course."

Sir Gorrann and Wardley were practically on top of her now, wiping and tending to the cuts on her head, her chin, and the various other wounds the king had given her. Mundoo emerged from the crowd of Yurkei behind her.

"The king is dead?" he asked.

"Yes," said Dinah, exhausted beyond measure.

Mundoo pulled a dagger from his belt and walked swiftly toward her. Dinah felt Sir Gorrann go rigid, his hand on his blade. Wardley stepped in front of her. Mundoo looked Dinah coldly in the eye, and when she didn't blink, he slapped her happily on the back before he knelt over the body. The king's head came off easily, and Mundoo raised it up in front of his troops, who exploded with cheers and hollers. Dinah turned away, nauseated.

"We must go," Cheshire whispered to Dinah. "Now. Wonderland Palace is falling."

Dinah walked out of the keep, leaving the king's headless body behind. Mundoo and his men followed with the king's head. The late king's men stayed behind in the keep.

"Where is Vittiore?" she asked Cheshire as they walked, Sir Gorrann fussing over the wound on her head. "Why wasn't she in the keep with the others?"

Cheshire smiled meanly. "She was hiding inside her bedroom, the coward. Some of the Spades have brought her down to the courtyard. We must act quickly. The Yurkei are within the walls and the people are restless. If we don't take control, this day will end with a ruined kingdom."

Dinah nodded, taking it all in, trying to wipe as much blood from herself as possible as they walked. Wardley trailed silently behind, looking grave and pale, as troubled as Dinah had ever seen him. *Perhaps the battle had changed him.* Dinah shook her head—of course, the battle would have changed them all.

She passed an open window near the palace library and heard the sounds of kingdom-wide panic raging outside—a morbid mix of weeping, whooping, and mad pleas. Though she had never been more exhausted, she began sprinting now, her legs pumping underneath her, the men running beside her. Together, they plunged through a maze of hallways and kitchens and porticos before exploding through the doorway to the main courtyard. The bright outside light temporarily blinded her, and she uttered a low cry when the world came into focus.

Thick black smoke filled the sky, the entire expanse of the palace simmering with its onyx hue. The world had turned into a hell. The stables—once her favorite place— had been burned to the ground. Hungry flames still licked at one large piece of the structure. Two slain Heart Cards lay in front of the stable, their uniforms beginning to glow with sparks. Yurkei were everywhere. Spades and Cards were fighting in the streets, the ring of their swords echoing up the buildings, their faces twisted with rage. The cries of her people were all around. The ground was littered with bodies and weapons, and terrified children sat huddled in corners, crying softly for their fathers. One lone Diamond Card stared blankly at the tallest turret of Wonderland Palace, paralyzed by shock.

War came at such a high cost. She thought she had understood it, but she hadn't. Not then. She did now. When the Spades saw her, they began shouting her name, happy to see her alive and well. The people of Wonderland stayed silent and watched her with eyes both fearful and full of rage.

In the center of the courtyard, hundreds of weary people waited in front of the execution platform. When they saw Dinah walking toward the platform, bloodied and holding the king's crown, they stepped back, creating a long, narrow aisle—just as they would for a queen. Dinah took a deep breath, instructing herself not to feel the thousands of eyes upon her and the weight of their safety on her shoulders.

"Wait!" Cheshire reached around her and placed the king's crown on her head. "You might need this. Now, listen to me. *Stand proud*. Look at them, like little sheep, waiting so desperately for a leader—any leader. The loyalty of these people is yours for the taking, so take it."

She began to walk up the aisle. Wardley reached out

from the crowd, looking frantic and terrified. His face was covered with sweat, and Dinah feared he was more wounded than he appeared. He roughly grabbed her waist, his eyes pleading.

"Dinah, whatever Cheshire said, be merciful. Stick to the plan. Vittiore is loved by the people. The king beheaded her mother in front of her. Grant her mercy. I beg of you, be the ruler that he was not. If you kill her, we will have a riot on our hands."

Dinah kissed him softly on the cheek. He gave a slight bow of his head, and she continued up the aisle, with Mundoo following a few steps behind. The Yurkei warrior held the king's head high above his own. As she made her way toward the front, Dinah could hear the painful gasps of her people as they saw the head of their former leader. It was cruel to show them, but necessary. She looked around the courtyard as she walked, her dark eyes wide with wonder.

The white roses were painted red. That was the first thing Dinah noticed as she strolled proudly toward the execution platform. The white garden roses, the ones she had lovingly planted with her mother so long ago, were spotted and slashed with drops of deep ruby. Blood was splattered across the white and black cobblestones, a deep crimson spreading across the sidewalks and gardens. The roses had gotten the worst of it, as evidenced by the many bodies that lay curled against the vine, as if these men were merely taking a nap in their fragrant blooms.

The soles of her boots were slick with blood and mud. Her sword bounced against her bruised hip as she walked. Thousands of nervous eyes followed her as she proceeded up the narrow aisle, their heads bowing to the ground as she approached. Dinah could smell their fear as she brushed past them. She was their queen now, and she would have their allegiance whether they gave it willingly or not.

The king's crown lay heavily on her head, its golden points digging into her skull and pulling on her thick black hair. She tried to hide that her steps trembled with exhaustion, and she was aware that she was probably covered in even more blood than the roses. When Dinah reached the stairway to the platform, she looked up at its giant obsidian steps. These steps led to a long block of white marble, a place where hundreds had lost their heads. As she lifted her foot to the first step, a drop of blood fell to the ground. She paused. The last thing she needed was to slip down the stairs in front of her new subjects. She was no longer that weak girl that they remembered. She turned to the nearest Card.

"Take off your cloak and wipe my boots," she barked. The young Heart Card fumbled with his clasp, his hands shaking as he yanked the cloak from around his shoulders.

"My queen." He knelt before her, taking her boots in his calloused hands and frantically wiping at the blood on the soles. She waited patiently for him to finish before climbing the staircase, her knees giving a slight tremble on each step. At long last, she stood on the platform, looking down at her new subjects as the rumbling cheers of her army shook the castle grounds. She savored the taste of victory on her tongue. It was a bittersweet flavor—hard-won and lovely at the same time. A hesitant smile crept over her lips. The last time she had seen this courtyard, she was running for her life. As she enjoyed the view of the smoldering castle, Vittiore's pathetic whimpering assaulted her eardrums.

"Please . . . ," she cried, her voice breaking over the now-hushed crowds. "Please, Dinah, you don't understand." Huge blue eyes, the color of cornflowers, peered up at her as the girl painfully lifted her head from the chopping block. She was so much more beautiful than Dinah had remembered. Her golden hair flowed over the white marble. It glowed now, radiant in the light. She was pale and small, adorned in a flowered gown. Only one shoe was left on her feet.

The queen raised her arms and the crowd fell silent. Cheshire was right—these people wanted someone to take charge of their lives, even if she had just attacked their city. Behind the girl, the trembling executioner stepped forward, stripped of his hood. His voice was shaking, but a poke from a Yurkei blade made his deep voice echo around the court-yard.

"Say it," the warrior hissed.

The executioner unrolled a sheet of paper covered in Cheshire's elaborate scroll.

"Vittiore, the once false queen, stands accused of the following offenses: high treason, sedition, and being an accessory to murder. You shall be judged and punished according to the Queen of Hearts, the only true queen."

The crowd cheered, egged on by Dinah's soldiers, who

raised their swords menacingly at her name. The girl dissolved into loud sobs, her tears dripping down the block.

"I'll tell you everything. Please, Dinah, you don't know what you are doing!" Her frail body began to shake as she melted into hysterics. "This must be a terrible dream, it must be." She repeated the phrase over and over again.

The executioner turned to Dinah, beads of sweat dripping into his eyes. "What is the queen's verdict, Your Majesty?" He gave Dinah a pained look.

Dinah raised her head and stared out past the crowd, past the devastated iron gates and the Black Towers, past the ashen ruins of the stables. The Queen of Hearts took a deep breath and looked out over the Wonderland Plains. The wide afternoon sky was breathtaking—dewy lavender and orange stretched out over heavy clouds as a blue storm gathered over the Twisted Wood. This was the day she'd dreamed of for so long, the power hers for the taking. The blood on her boots was almost dry, and she finally had all she wanted. Vengeance was hers, at long last.

The blond-haired, blue-eyed girl raised her head again, a look of desperation marring her radiant face.

"Please!" she screamed.

Dinah should be merciful. She would be merciful. She had made a promise. She wasn't like him. She paused, eyeing the crowd. She knew how to earn their love, but how to best seal their fear without becoming a tyrant?

"OFF WITH HER HEAD!" she screamed.

"No!" yelled Wardley, who was now standing nervously behind the platform. "Dinah, no!"

Sir Gorrann gestured for Dinah to stop, and even Cheshire, who was watching the crowd with his narrow cat eyes, frowned with concern. The executioner took a tentative step toward his ax, and then another. With shaking hands, he stepped beside the dethroned queen. The crowd grew wild and restless, shouting and begging for mercy as they pushed against each other, and against the Spades who surrounded them.

Dinah watched them, her dark eyes calculating and careful. The executioner clasped the ax low over Vittiore's neck and she grew oddly silent, her eyes trained on something Dinah couldn't see. Her perfect pink lips were forming silent sentences. The executioner raised the ax above Vittiore's head, preparing to strike, something he had done thousands of times. He took a breath, squared his shoulders, and shifted the ax for the fatal blow.

Dinah suddenly raised her hand.

"Stop!" she barked at the executioner. The crowd was still, their hands folded in prayer, every eye upon her. Dinah cleared her throat. "I will grant her mercy, only because you have asked it of me, and because mercy is the mark of a great leader, something you have never known with the King of Hearts. Vittiore does not deserve mercy, for she sat upon a throne that was not hers. This woman is no relation to the king, Queen Davianna, nor me or my deceased brother, Charles. She is a traitor, a conspirator, a stranger who ruled over you. By all of Wonderland laws, she deserves death, for that is the punishment for her crimes. And yet, I hope you will see that I am not like your murderous King of Hearts, a man who killed his own son and blamed it on his daughter in order not to share his throne."

Her people gave a loud gasp, followed by whispered conversation. *Could this be true?*

"I promise you this. I have come to rule over you not

with fear, but with patience and strength. I would ask that you give me your loyalty, to rebuild this city, to make a better Wonderland for all of us and our neighbors, the Yurkei. They are not the people you have been taught to fear, but rather a peaceful and generous race. . . ." Dinah cringed, wishing for a moment that Mundoo was not holding the king's disembodied head beside her.

"I will strive for peace and commerce with our neighbors, all of them! The Yurkei have much to teach us, and as an act of good faith, when this day is done they will leave the palace walls and reside outside on the Wonderland Plains until our work and treaties here are done."

Dinah looked up and saw Sir Gorrann watching her silently, his expression bursting with pride, his eyes blurred with tears. Dinah's own voice caught in her throat as she raised a bloody hand above her head. She could feel it. The crowd was hers.

"I vow to you this day that I will be the ruler that the King of Hearts never was. I vow to you that criminals will have their day in court before being shut away in the Black Towers. I vow that people who speak up about injustice will not simply disappear. If we are ever attacked again, I vow that I will open the palace for your protection. And when I am done making sure that this palace and city are put back to their former glory, I swear as the daughter of Davianna, the Queen of Hearts, that I will empty the Black Towers. The evil that rots this palace from below will be flushed out and we will look to a time when Wonderland enters a peaceful period of prosperity. Will you join me?"

The crowd erupted in wild, tear-filled cheers.

Dinah raised her chin. "Release her."

The executioner helped Vittiore up from the white marble block. Her face was tearstained and weary. She fell at Dinah's feet and kissed them, as her blond hair washed around Dinah's boots.

"Thank you, thank you, you are my queen, you are my queen."

Dinah turned away from Vittiore and walked swiftly down the platform steps toward the crowd. Her new subjects reached out for her, begging to touch her hands, her face, her feet. She smiled at each one of them, her bloodied hands brushing many, her cracked lips gracing the heads of plump babies, now safe. A shower of roses, plucked from the bushes around them, fell around her like rain.

"All hail the Queen of Hearts! All hail the Queen of Hearts!"

Dinah shut her eyes and let the glory sweep over her. For just a moment, the world was hers. *Thank the gods that humans are so fickle.* Cheshire had been right about everything. By granting Vittiore mercy, she had won the people. *Our plan worked.*

Cheshire marched up beside her. "Your Grace. My Queen. We should get you cleaned up before you begin restoring order. A queen shouldn't be covered with such filth. More important, your wounds need tending."

"I have one last thing to do first," she answered, walking quickly now so that Cheshire ran to keep up.

"May I be of assistance?" he asked.

"No."

This was something she needed to do alone.

♥

Dinah flung open the doors to the Black Towers, letting light flood into the darkness. This time, she would not be sneaking in through the underground tunnels. The towers were barely manned; a few nervous Clubs had been left to linger behind. News traveled fast in Wonderland, and they bowed to her as she entered. She grabbed one and pushed him up against the wall.

"Where is he?" she hissed. The guard pointed to the top of the tower, and Dinah ran faster than she had run through the castle, spiraling up and up and up until she was dizzy and her breathing labored. Up one circle and then up one more, she climbed her way up through the levels of the hive, an unending spiral that reeked of death. The highest-ranking Club in the Towers tried to keep up with her, but he was several floors below her before long. Dirty hands, some twisted with slimy black roots, reached out for her as she passed their cells. *Soon*, she thought, *soon I will come back for all of you.*

"It's the queen! It's the Queen of Hearts!" one yelled, and soon the whole prison was filled with catcalls and the cheers of the insane.

Dinah reached the top level. It was tiny, barely ten feet across and black as night. There was a padlock around some iron bars: a new silver padlock, perfect for a heart-shaped key. Dinah yanked at the doors, desperate. They clanged loudly as she shook them. She screamed at the guard.

"Unlock this door or I swear I will have your head!"

The Club fumbled with the keys, dropping them twice on the grime-covered floor before Dinah grabbed them from his hand. Finally, she found the heart-shaped key and pushed it inside the lock, flinging wide the cell doors. She saw the outline of a body, curled over on a bench. A gnarled beard and a knotty spine rose and fell with each breath.

He was much thinner than she remembered. His face was hidden by the dark, but his voice was so familiar—warm and loving.

"Who's there?" it called out. "Who is it? I can't see!"

Dinah walked forward and motioned for the guard to bring the lantern over. The prisoner was gaunt, with black circles under his eyes, and the lean look of hunger was etched into his cheeks. His hands shook as he covered his eyes.

"Who is it? Please, no more, I beg of you!"

She was silent for a moment and then bent down and touched his face gently with the palm of her hand. "Harris?"

A cry escaped his lips. "Dinah?" He reached out to touch her bruised face, her blood-soaked hair.

She released a sob. "I'm here." She took his dear, withered old face in her hands and looked upon it with love. "I am queen now, and you will never set foot in this tower again, old friend."

Harris cried out again and pressed his cracked lips against her palms. "My child, I knew you were alive. I could feel it! The roots told me that you were alive! They whispered it to me when I slept. I saw you in my dreams. I saw you in a field of mushrooms, saw you take the shape of a crane. . . ."

She did not doubt it for a second. He raised his eyes to hers, and Dinah saw a glimpse of the old Harris, jovial and gay, staring back at her in rapturous joy. She took his arm in hers.

"Will you give me one honor?" he whispered.

"Anything," she replied.

"Step away from me."

Dinah stepped back in confusion and Harris very slowly pushed himself up from the stone bench. He stumbled twice, and Dinah reached out to catch him. His legs and chest shook with the effort of standing, but he batted her hands away.

"Do not help me, child!" he said sternly.

Dinah moved away from him, unsure of what to do. Harris gave her a smile with blackened teeth.

"I have been waiting to do this since I pulled you screaming from your mother's womb. Wild and angry even then." He paused. "Perfect to me, even then." With a happy sob, he tenderly bowed before her. "My queen. How may I serve you?"

His legs collapsed beneath him, and Dinah eased him back onto the stone bench. He placed his gentle hand on her head, his voice a lullaby that she had dearly missed.

"Be at peace, my dear. Rest finally."

Dinah then bent her face into his lap and wept unabashedly for all she had seen and done.

Eleven

Dinah looked at herself in the gilded mirror, preparing for the coronation that would crown her queen. She frowned at the thought. It seemed like a lifetime ago that she had killed the king, and yet it had only been four days since the end of the war. The barrage of events that had followed had occurred with such urgency that time had passed quickly.

As soon as peace had been declared and the fighting stopped, Dinah had sent the Yurkei just outside the palace walls to await their release back to Hu-Yuhar. Mundoo remained in the palace, to make sure that Dinah kept her promises and to see her through the coronation, just in case some faction of leftover Cards attempted a revolt.

It was all for naught—there was not a whisper of discontent. The Yurkei and the Spades outnumbered the Cards two to one, and any talk of insurgency would have been a swift walk down the road to death.

Dinah was amazed at and grateful for how quickly Cheshire was able to organize everything—laws, ordinances, titles, and land were all distributed within two days of Dinah declaring herself queen. The result was a sigh of relief from both the people and the Yurkei, who longed to return to their peaceful lives at Hu-Yuhar. Part of Dinah wished she could go with them, live out her life at Hu-Yuhar under the watchful eye of the cranes and Mundoo, who was the kind of leader that Dinah aspired to be. It wouldn't be the same without Bah-kan, though, and Dinah knew that her soul belonged here, in the palace.

She clutched her hands together, feeling her nerves getting the better of her. Overthrow and kill a king? Fine.

Stand in front of all her new subjects in a dress? Terrifying.

The entirety of Wonderland proper had been invited to the coronation. People stretched out through the Great Hall and into the hallways and stairwells of Wonderland Palace. The high-born members of the court and the low farmhands, the famous and the decorated, spilled out into the courtyard. All longed to see the Queen of Hearts, who had gone from an embodiment of terror to the hero of the people. Their fickle hearts made Dinah uneasy, but Cheshire had explained their motivations away as he helped prepare her for the coronation.

She turned back to him now as he sat in the queen's reading chair across the room, his dazzling new purple cloak a burst of color against the soft brown leather. He lazily twirled his dagger in his right hand.

Dinah's bedroom was in shambles, but pieces of her old life remained: a trinket here, a music box or book there. Eventually, these chambers would be glorious, but right now they were little more than a makeshift dressing room.

"Are you listening, Your Majesty?"

Dinah turned back. "Yes. I'm just . . . thinking."

Cheshire cleared his throat and continued on with his

lecture about the coronation. "Remember this. Peasants and regular townspeople care not for the business of kings and queens. They long for stability above all. Unless your war killed one of their family members, in which case you will probably be their sworn enemy forever, don't worry about their loyalty. These people want to tend to their farms, have their babies, eat their tarts, and live in peace. To them now, you are a fascinating woman, a source of rich gossip, and they want nothing more than to see you take the throne. The masses love to see a leader brought low, and you have given them that. Now they simply wish to discuss what dress you wear, what you say, what you eat, what you do."

Cheshire stood and handed her a short speech on a rolled scroll.

"This should rouse them sufficiently after the coronation is over. I'll give you a minute to get dressed."

As he walked out, the doors to Dinah's airy chambers burst open, and three maids struggled in with an enormous dress wrapped delicately in bright purple linen. Dinah looked at the dress and sighed. She already missed her boots, her tunic, and her wool pants. The people expected a queen to dress a certain way and so she would, but she would never throw away the muddy, bloody boots that sat beside her bed. Those were the boots that had walked the vast reaches of Wonderland, and the blood crusted on their sides had come at a great cost.

Vittiore ducked her blond head inside the room and gave Dinah a timid smile. With reluctance, Dinah had hired Vittiore as her lady-in-waiting, a more suitable post for a girl born on the Western Slope. This was at the urging of Wardley, who had taken pity on the skinny waif. People were drawn to her glow the way insects buzzed around a wilting flower. Dinah could barely understand it, but she hesitantly allowed Vittiore to serve her. There were some things only they shared: both had been manipulated by the king. He had killed both of their mothers. It bonded them without words.

Vittiore motioned silently for the maids to hang Dinah's dress by the window. The maids bowed to Dinah, who gave them a gentle nod before letting them scuttle out of her vast chamber. Only Ki-ershan, Vittiore, and Dinah remained.

Ki-ershan, who had been inseparable from Dinah since the battle, stood by the door at the far side of the room. He had exchanged his loincloth for a tunic bearing Dinah's seal, but the white stripes that ran from his blue eyes to the end of his feet remained. Ki-ershan was everything she had ever wanted in a guard—he was crafty and intuitive, and knew what she needed before she did. He sensed danger before it was present and had already provided her with wise counsel. He helped Dinah look over treaties and ledgers in her room, well after the rest of Wonderland had turned to their pillows.

Vittiore bowed her head. "We're ready, Your Majesty."

Ki-ershan turned his head.

With a grimace, Dinah stepped out of her dressing gown and stood naked before the mirror, staring at herself. Her lean, muscular form was so different from the stout and soft body she had left behind. *So many scars*, she thought as her black eyes took in the damaged form before her. One large scar ran across the back of her shoulder where Mundoo had "reminded" her of his power. A jagged wound crossed her palm where she had pulled a bone spike out of Morte's leg. It had never healed correctly. Neither had her two fingers, which were still a bit crooked. The wide gash across her chin remained, as well as the wound on her head, bruised, sore, and still occasionally leaking. A gift from the King of Hearts.

Vittiore began gently taping a linen wrap over her torso. Cheshire believed Dinah had cracked a rib when the Club had pushed her off Morte. She winced. It was tender to the touch.

"Be careful," murmured Vittiore, touching Dinah's side gently, her small hand just below Dinah's breast. "You're still healing."

Dinah looked at her reflection as Vittiore stood next to her, fussing over her rib. Vittiore was wearing a simple, pale-pink dress, and yet she radiated light. It was like standing next to a doll, next to something unreal and holy. Next to her, Dinah felt like a living wound, compressed into one compact form. Still, she allowed a smile to stretch across her face. She had earned these scars, and she was queen after all of it.

I would choose victory over beauty any day.

She sat still as Vittiore applied rouge to her face and drew a tiny heart underneath her right eye—a symbol of her loyalty to the Cards.

"Draw another one," Dinah ordered, pointing to her other eye. "Put the Spade symbol here."

"Are you sure, Your Majesty?"

"Yes. I will show the people that Starey Belft did not die in vain."

Vittiore cupped her tiny hand under Dinah's chin, lifting it ever so slightly. Her fingers trembling, she drew the tiny Spade symbol with a black charcoal pencil. Her blue eyes, the color of an early morning sea, looked with genuine care upon Dinah's face. Loving Vittiore as a sister might be easier than Dinah had originally thought. Vittiore dashed bright red lipstick across Dinah's heart mouth.

"All right, we're done. Let's get your dress on."

With a gasp, Vittiore lifted Dinah's coronation gown out of its purple linen wrap and laid it on the bed. Fifty seamstresses, with a fair wage from the queen's new discretionary fund, had stitched this dress together in three days. Dinah refused to wear the gown that had adorned Vittiore, and so a new coronation dress had been designed by Cheshire, a man of seemingly endless talents. The bottom of the dress was bone white, decorated with thousands of tiny red hearts. The tip of each red heart collided with the top of another, and so the gown resembled a spider web of red hearts, each dotted with a single tiny ruby. The top of the gown was bloodred, and made to cinch perfectly to Dinah's figure. The signs of the Cards—Hearts, Diamonds, Clubs, and Spades—ran across the bustline before it arched up over Dinah's shoulders. The back of the bodice was made of just the red heart webbing, showing a scandalous amount of Dinah's shoulders and lower back. The base of the skirt was dusted in a shimmering white, so that when Dinah walked up the aisle, the fabric would sparkle and dance. She would look as if she were walking on air.

Dinah stepped delicately into the dress as Vittiore raised it up over her shoulders. Dinah felt all the air in the room get sucked away as Vittiore began binding the corset that pressed hard against Dinah's broken rib. She bit down on her lip.

"I'm so sorry, Your Majesty," whispered Vittiore. "I can loosen it if you desire."

"No."

Vittiore's speech faded into hazy mumbling as Dinah stared at herself in the mirror, encouraged by what she saw. For a moment, Dinah looked just like her mother.

"We must go, Your Majesty. Your escort is ready and the walk is quite long."

Dinah let a deep breath of air fill her chest, which pressed painfully into her corset. She winced. The dress was so heavy that she was having a hard time standing in it. Vittiore laid her hand gently on Dinah's side and tucked a stray lock of Dinah's hair back into place.

"Breathe, but not too deeply. Don't injure your rib further."

Dinah gave a nod and turned away from her. "I'm ready."

"You look like a queen," the girl said softly.

♥

Dinah walked alone through the hallway, turned the corner, and gasped.

At the end of the long corridor, which shimmered with the light of hundreds of pink torches, Sir Gorrann waited, dressed in his finest Spade uniform, all polished and clean.

He was almost unrecognizable. The Spade bowed deeply when she approached. The new commander of the Cards took Dinah's free arm.

"I barely recognize you, sir."

He gave a deep laugh. "And yeh as well. That dress probably weighs more than yeh do. It's honestly a bit ridiculous."

Dinah gave his arm a squeeze. "I like it. I look like my mother."

The Spade kept his eyes trained straight ahead as they walked through the stone corridors of the palace, the filtered red light of the heart windows beaming over their bright faces.

"Dinah, sometimes I forget how young yeh are still. Yeh always thought yeh would share the throne with yer father, at least until yeh were married. Yeh were never supposed to rule alone."

"Ruling alone is better than ruling beside a tyrant."

"True, but being a queen is much more complicated than yeh know. Hopefully, yeh'll do a better job than the King of Hearts did."

"I will," whispered Dinah, though a pang of doubt twisted through her. The King of Hearts might not be her actual father, but deep inside, she still felt the rage that had driven him. It scared her. She had grown up in its presence, and now it had infected her like a virus.

Dinah and Sir Gorrann were in the Hallway of the Golden Birds now, each metal fowl gazing down at her accusingly as their living kin fluttered around the rafters and skipped across the floor.

"This is where I leave you." Sir Gorrann bowed and kissed her hand. "I have not seen a day this beautiful since I held my girls in my arms." He stood up and winked. "Don't sneeze in that dress, or yeh'll be showing everyone what's special about the Queen of Hearts."

Dinah snickered and hit his arm. "Go."

With a deep breath, she turned, knowing who waited for her.

Standing in front of a stuffed peacock, Wardley waited patiently for his queen. Dinah felt a stone rise up in her throat at the sight of him, so handsome in his new Knave of Hearts uniform, several new seals pressed across his cloak. Wardley looked over at her, gazed at his friend with misty eyes full of pride. Dinah squeezed his hand. There was so much she wanted to tell him, so much she wished he would say, but they were on opposite sides of a chasm so great it would swallow them whole. Dinah let out a long breath.

"Are you ready?" she whispered, but what she had meant to say was, *Could you try to love me? Just a little.*

With a kind smile, Wardley moved her hand and took her arm.

His face was so proud, the jagged scar on his cheek still dark and angry. Like Dinah's body, half of his face was shadowed with healing bruises. Dinah stifled a laugh.

"What could you possibly be laughing at right now?" Wardley whispered to her.

"At what a motley bunch we are. Bruised and bloody, and about to enter the Great Hall."

"It does seem strange that just four days ago we were knee deep in blood. So many dead."

They paused, brutal memories ripping through them both. Finally, Wardley took a step forward, pulling Dinah with him, overtly changing the subject.

"I must tell you that your dress is utterly ridiculous. It's the size of a house!"

"Really?" Dinah did a playful twirl. "I have to admit, I think I quite like it."

"You? Liking a dress? I'll believe it when I see it. Did they not have a coronation tunic on hand for today?"

"No, but if I would have asked for one, Cheshire would have had it made within an hour."

Wardley shook his head. "Isn't that the sad truth?"

They laughed together until they stood in front of the vast golden doors that separated them from thousands of eyes. Harris was there, waiting like a father on her wedding day. He bowed, but not without difficulty. He had made incredible progress since Dinah had come for him in the Black Towers: the ruddiness in his cheeks had returned, and he had put on a few pounds since then. He was still painfully thin, and the dark gouges beneath his eyes lingered. But the joy that leaped out from them this day overpowered any sorrow drifting around him.

Harris clasped Dinah's hands in his own and kissed

both of her cheeks. "Finally." Tears sprang to his eyes as he hugged her tightly. "The day I have dreamed about for so long is finally here. Are you ready, my queen?"

Dinah looked at the golden doors, remembering the last time she had stood here. It was the day her father had brought Vittiore into her life, the day that his violent grasp for power had begun. She had fought her way back to this place, and now, she would enter not as an abused child but as a woman.

As a queen.

She nodded. "I'm ready." Wardley and Sir Gorrann pulled open the wide doors, and a chorus rose through the air, a song Dinah had not heard since childhood.

Ah, cruel three! In such an hour,
Beneath such dreamy weather,
To beg a tale of breath too weak
To stir the tiniest feather!
Yet what can one poor voice avail
Against three tongues together?

Anon, to sudden silence won,

In fancy they pursue

The dream-child moving through a land

Of wonders wild and new,

In friendly chat with bird or beast—

And half believe it true.

And ever, as the story drained

The wells of fancy dry,

And faintly strove that weary one

To put the subject by,

"The rest next time—" "It is next time!"

The happy voices cry.

Thus grew the tale of Wonderland:

Thus slowly, one by one,

Its quaint events were hammered out—

And now the tale is done,

And home we steer, a merry crew,

Beneath the setting sun.

Painted doves, each swirled with glistening scenes too beautiful to linger on, were released to symbolize the arrival of the new queen. They were joined by a few white cranes from the Yurkei, a nod of support for Dinah. Vast swaths of white and red linen draped the domed ceiling, waving in the light breeze that caressed the crowd. Harris kissed her hand and let her go with a wink. *We did it.*

She took a tentative step up the impossibly long aisle, and then another. A pair of red jeweled slippers, her mother's design, carried her down the aisle. As she walked the bloodred carpet toward the throne, her subjects bowed before her, a pleasure that never got old. Seemingly endless showers of rose petals fell upon her head. The choir of young boys raised their voices together until they formed one long, lonely note, a melancholy sound used for the ending of an age. Dinah reminded herself to breathe.

Mundoo and Cheshire waited for her at the end of the aisle, flanking the throne. They were surrounded by dozens of cloaked lords and the local clergy, each wearing their finest black robes. When Dinah reached them, Cheshire bowed and Mundoo simply gave a nod of his head. This was a gesture to show not only Dinah but the people of Wonderland that Mundoo was not one of her subjects but rather her equal. Mundoo looked resplendent in his full headdress of feathers and an intricately woven robe dotted with tiny stitched mountains. It shifted in the bright afternoon light. Cheshire wore his purple cloak, now adorned with dozens of sparkling brooches. The most powerful man in Wonderland had a need for everyone to know his position.

Dinah reached the throne, her breath catching in her throat, crushed under a wave of happiness and the weight of her dress. There they were, the pair of gold thrones, cut from the same metal as Mundoo's throne in Hu-Yuhar. Each was shaped like one large heart. They were embellished at the top with a cascade of rising hearts, each one razor sharp and more folded than the next. The throne next to her sat empty, with only a white rose placed on it—a single rose to hold that place until she married.

Dinah climbed the stone steps she had knelt before so many times and turned to face the crowd. As she looked down upon her subjects, she was crushed by a surprising wave of gratitude and love. Standing here, in the place that was always destined for her, Dinah's soul was sailing. She raised her hand and the crowd grew silent. Dinah stared at each of them, a dazzling smile upon her radiant face, before sitting upon her throne.

The ceremony began, an intricate and ancient set of rituals with many readings, proclamations, stories, and songs. It took hours. Dinah stood and sat repeatedly while affirming each and every clause and duty of the queen. Each one she stored in her heart, convinced that each pledge of fealty would make her a better queen, a better leader, than those who had come before her.

At the end of the lengthy ceremony—Dinah noticed some children in the first row nodding off—the four commanders of the Cards approached her, each carrying a gold tray displaying a single playing card. Wardley and Sir Gorrann stood between the new commander of the Clubs and the new commander of the Diamonds, who was still nursing a thigh wound. All bowed before her, their trays outstretched. Cheshire stepped before the queen holding a single pearl-headed needle. Dinah gave her finger, which he cradled in a red felt cloth. Then he brought the needle down into her finger, much harder than Dinah believed was necessary. She didn't make a sound as he withdrew it and a dot of warm blood pooled on the tip. He stepped aside as each of the four Cards brought up his tray and playing card. Dinah leaned forward and pressed her blood onto the surface of each card, one by one. The Cards were covered with dozens of other bloody fingerprints, from the kings and queens who had come before her. When it was Wardley's turn, he gave her a sly smile. It was as if a thin shard of glass had been deftly inserted into her heart. She ignored it, giving him a shy smile in return. Nothing would take this day from her.

The Cards bowed before the throne and parted to the sides, their role in the ceremony complete. The chorus of voices rose again, in a holy song about kings and queens of old. The crowd fell to their knees as Vittiore began her walk up the aisle, humbled and stripped of her royalty, wearing a very plain dress for such a high ceremony. She carried the crown upon a deep-fuchsia pillow, only it was not the crown that Dinah was expecting.

It was *her* crown. The base was a brushed silver, inlaid with thousands of tiny heart gemstones. She remembered the flowered vines that twisted out from the hearts to meet at the top of the crown. The vines were carved with tiny faces, their mouths open in a scream. Flickering stars hung from thin strips of silver among the vines. The strips of silver were the same tree trunks that greeted her inside the Twisted Wood. Four Card symbols connected the vines from the sides of the crown to the top, where a diamond in the shape of a heart sparkled in the light, framed by the outline of a crane.

Dinah closed her eyes and saw Charles before her, his blue and green eyes peering up at her with curiosity. His small hands, his tiny body cradled against her own. She remembered the smell of his dirty blond hair, streaked with grease and paint. He was here with her, she could feel it. This was Charles's crown for Dinah, something she assumed the king had destroyed. The entire room went silent and still, and it seemed only Vittiore was moving, bringing the crown closer. The crown itself was so beautiful that people reached out to touch it, breaking protocol. Charles's crown, his last gift to Dinah. She felt her heart shredding and forced her face to remain frozen as she watched the last remnant of her brother come up the aisle.

Dinah blinked rapidly, trying to remain in control. Vittiore stood before her now, the crown held aloft in her trembling hands, a show to the people that their once queen was truly submitting to Dinah, the new Queen of Hearts. Vittiore circled around behind Dinah, handing the crown to Cheshire, who slowly lowered the heavy crown onto Dinah's head. Silent tears spilled from Dinah's eyes as the crown settled across her brow, the presence of her brother so close now. She stood in front of her people and placed her hand over her heart.

Cheshire stood, proclaiming, "Wonderland, behold your queen, the Queen of Hearts!"

The crowd repeated the phrase back to him, and then took up the chant, again and again. The choir sang and birds fluttered in the afternoon breeze. Her brother's crown sat firmly against her head, exquisitely measured so that it lay snug and tight across her brow. A perfect fit to rule.

Q
♥

Twelve

Though she was exhausted beyond measure and dreaming of her bed, Dinah hosted Mundoo in her chambers immediately following the coronation, hoping to finalize the remaining details of the peace treaty. Mundoo arrived with his personal guard in tow, and Dinah watched them with utter fascination. They were completely out of place inside the palace walls, uncomfortable and twitchy, suffocated by the stone walls and the red-tinted light. She saw two of the Yurkei quietly making faces at themselves in one of her ornate gilded mirrors, and several of them had planted themselves at her long table, helping themselves to a delicious array of new flavors. It was obvious to her that the Yurkei thought that Wonderlanders were excessive and ridiculous, just as fluttery and shallow as the birds that roamed the palace hallways. She smiled as she watched them. They weren't exactly wrong.

Mundoo leaned toward her, a cup of tea in his hand. "Shall we go to the balcony, Dinah?"

It was jarring to hear her name, now that everyone called her "Your Majesty" or some other lofty title. Mundoo was making a point; she wasn't his queen. She nodded and opened the doors to the balcony, light swallowing them as they stepped outside. The day was clear, and the Yurkei Mountains could be seen through the heavy summer air. Mundoo sipped his tea as Dinah watched him enviously; he wore his responsibilities with such an intense grace.

From here, Dinah could see the tents of Mundoo's remaining army lingering in the fields just outside of Wonderland proper, ready to depart at a moment's notice. They wanted to go home. As a show of kindness to the people of Wonderland, the tireless Yurkei had cleared out the wreckage of battle that lay smoldering around the castle, including the corpses. The bodies of Wonderlanders and Cards were burned, their ashes buried in the cemetery west of the palace, while the bodies of Yurkei warriors were set aside for the Caterpillar. After he had blessed the bodies, a small bone from their arms was removed and wrapped in white linen. These men's bones would be buried with the rest of their tribe in the mushroom fields outside Hu-Yuhar, their souls bonded forever with the land. Dinah understood there was no greater honor. What remained of their bodies was then taken to the Twisted Wood for burial.

The chief of the Yurkei leaned over the balcony, his bright blue eyes on the field below, the white and blue feathers in his hair blowing softly.

"Morte hasn't been found yet, I assume."

Dinah rested her arms on the stone terrace. "No. Only Keres was found, but you know that already."

Mundoo breathed in the steam of the tea. "This means you won't be able to uphold your end of the deal you made to save his life—the promise to give me six of his offspring—so we will have to make other arrangements. Another sacrifice."

Dinah turned to him with skepticism in her eyes. "I will

not budge on the treaty, so don't ask."

Mundoo smiled at her before turning back to his cup.

"Actually, I was going to ask to have regular shipments of tea to Hu-Yuhar. My warriors can't get enough of it."

Dinah felt a jolt of satisfaction. Every morning she had sent jittery servants out with heaping trays of tea to placate the waiting tribe. It was a tiny gesture, but she had learned that even the most subtle gift of service could influence the people.

"Be careful, Chief. Once you have a drink of it, it becomes something you need more and more of just to sustain yourself through the day."

The chief looked to the mountains. "It's the same with power."

Silence encompassed the balcony as Dinah weighed his words.

Mundoo cleared his throat.

"From here, our mountains seem so insignificant, just small hills that mark . . . what is your Wonderland word for it . . . the end of the sky? The beyond? It's a good one, but I can't remember it."

Dinah clasped her hands behind her back. "The horizon?"

"Yes, yes, that's it. The horizon. It is a lovely thing, is it not? And yet, it is not so far from here to there. Not so far for many men who can ride without ceasing."

Dinah raised her eyebrow. "Is that a threat?"

Mundoo's blazing blue eyes looked back at her, unnerving in their direct gaze. "A threat? No. Let's just call it a reminder. Dinah, we are a peaceful people, as you know. We belong to the land, and she to us. We have no desire for war." He took another sip of his apple-blossom tea. "I have seen too much death, Queen of Hearts. I am weary of coronations, councils, meetings, and treaties. My mountains are calling to me, and my warriors long for their warm beds and the wives that keep them that way. We will depart from here now, with the treaty intact. As agreed upon, in a few months a large group of my people will arrive at Ierladia to tour the city that will be our stronghold. As you requested, the city will not be touched, but I fear that our presence there may cause some alarm. Should this happen, my warriors will have no choice but to defend themselves."

Dinah rested her palms on the balcony railing. From here, she could see the scorched earth where the stables had been, her childhood replaced by ash and blackened dirt. She turned to Mundoo, her black eyes swallowing his whole. He wasn't the only one with power now.

"And that is why I plan to make the trip to Ierladia when it comes time to turn over the city. I will stand by my people and make sure that no one is hurt or taken advantage of when the Yurkei settlers arrive. In the same way, I hope to show that the Yurkei are a good people and should be trusted. If we are to share a city, we must make the example."

Mundoo stared back at her, unflinching but impressed. "You must know that I long for peace, truly," he stated plainly.

Dinah nodded. "I believe that you do. But I also believe that you see my city now, with so few Cards to defend us, and we must look like a shiny new toy, so tempting and vulnerable. However, in a few months, you will find a new Wonderland proper, and a host of willing Cards who will be trained for battle, better men than those my father led. You will find new walls, this time made of stone and not iron.

And you will find a queen who is not so easily breakable."

With a calm breath, Dinah cautiously reached for his hand. "I value a peace with the Yurkei above all other treaties and measures. Believe that I came to love your tribe and your city, and I would bemoan any loss to your people as much as my own."

Her eyes fell on Ki-ershan, who stood rigidly in the corner of the room. His eyes were trained on Mundoo, his hands flexed tightly around his sword. Mundoo smiled bitterly at him. He dropped her hand and put both of his palms on Dinah's shoulders, looking as though he wanted to give her a friendly squeeze. Or, that was how it was meant to appear. Only Dinah could feel his finger pressing against her scar, the one he had given her with his thin knife. She stifled a cry of pain as his fingers probed and pushed, willing herself to remain strong. Mundoo's tea-soaked breath washed over her face

"Do not forget our treaty, Queen of Hearts. Should you break your promises, raid our lands, or kill my people, I will burn this palace to the ground along with all those in it. Respect the boundaries bestowed by the treaty, and I promise to do the same. I expect that you will visit Hu-Yuhar in a year's time to celebrate our happy arrangement. The tribe will be glad to see you."

Dinah could feel her vision tunneling as pain ricocheted up her arm, but she kept her face without emotion.

"As I will be to see them." She pushed Mundoo away roughly and raised her hand to dismiss him.

"I wish you safe travels to Hu-Yuhar. Wonderland Palace is grateful for your help in placing me on the throne."

"You had better keep it," Mundoo warned. "Do not trust anyone here. You are a good ruler, Dinah, and the queen this land deserves. Don't let it be taken away from you. And don't become your father. If that happens . . ." He shook his head and backed away, pulling a single feather from his headdress.

"Remember that day when our words blended together in sweat. Remember the cranes that bore witness. Remember our peace and our people. We are of the same land, brothers and sisters." He placed the feather in his hand and stretched out his open palm. "Good-bye, Queen of Hearts."

Dinah took the feather from his hand and turned away from him, letting him see the back that wouldn't be broken.

"I'll arrange a tea shipment as soon as things settle here."

She walked him to the very edge of the palace gates, Kiershan following behind them. Mundoo gave Dinah's hand a squeeze as he departed through the broken gates. A whooping cheer rose up from the Yurkei, chilling the blood of every Wonderlander. Dinah turned and climbed the stairs to the turret that overlooked the northern end of the castle. The remaining Yurkei army had their horses already mounted. Dinah raised her hand and her chin to say good-bye, and at Mundoo's nod, the Yurkei warriors held up their hands in the shape of a crane in return. She felt grateful tears welling in her eyes as she looked down at the people she had grown to love.

Mundoo mounted Keres, his flank striped blue for victory, his flaxen mane adorned with feathers. The chief of the Yurkei tribe gave a slight kick and Keres, massive even from where Dinah was standing, reared up on his hind legs. Mundoo lifted his sword in a gesture of both gratitude and warning to Dinah. With that, Keres turned and began to sprint west, to the Twisted Wood, back toward the hills and the winged stone guardians of Hu-Yuhar. The Yurkei army followed, and soon they were nothing more than a swiftly moving plume of dust, the very vision of speed.

Wonderland proper filled with the sound of thunder as the floor planks beneath Dinah's feet vibrated. Dozens of Cards peered through the twisted and deformed iron gates, watching the vanishing Yurkei with awe and relief. A few tiny children chased after the Yurkei, running behind the last of their army with makeshift wooden horses held high in the air. Dinah smiled. The adults of Wonderland might never lose their prejudices against the Yurkei, but the next generation would see them as wondrous and mysterious men, especially since roughly twenty Yurkei remained behind in Wonderland to maintain diplomatic relations.

Cheshire suddenly materialized beside her, and they watched silently as the Yurkei disappeared over the horizon. Once they were gone, he cleared his throat. "Your Majesty. If I may have your ear for a moment . . ."

Dinah frowned. "Cheshire, you always are in my ear."

He gave a soft chuckle, tinged with malice. "You possess such a quick wit, just like your mother."

"Thank you for the compliment. What is your concern?

Do we not have council tonight?"

"We do, but there are some things that require your immediate attention."

Strange, Dinah thought—she felt oddly uneasy with the Yurkei gone. To the people of Wonderland, their presence was an occupation, a dark threat outside their gates. To Dinah, they had been a reassurance, a protector. She sighed and turned to Cheshire. "Walk with me. I hear the groundskeepers are beginning repairs on the Croquet Lawn. Shall we go see?"

Cheshire bowed. "Nothing would please me more."

They carefully descended the steep wooden stairs of the turret and began making their way through the outlying business districts.

"Now, tell me what requires my attention most."

"First, Your Majesty, do you still plan on marrying Wardley in a few months' time? Though we have given him his due titles, I am still not sure that he is the correct choice to sit on the throne beside you."

"And why not?"

"He is not of royal blood, for one. His family is of noble

birth, but there are much more deserving lords and ladies who have a wealth of sons, all longing to marry the seductive black-eyed queen."

Dinah stayed silent, her hands sweaty underneath her plum-colored gown.

"Gambling on one of these young men, who would add handsomely to the treasury, might be worth your consideration."

Dinah grumbled under her breath. Cheshire continued.

"There is also the question of *heirs*. Should you marry Wardley, would it be a marriage that would produce sons and daughters to take the throne after you? Forgive me for speaking frankly, but if you choose Wardley for your king, am I correct in assuming that it would be a marriage of"— he paused—"friendship?"

Dinah stopped walking as shame overtook her, and her face burned with embarrassment. She whirled on Cheshire. "You step outside your bounds, sir. Wardley will be my king. This was decided in our treaty with the Yurkei. We would not do well to change our plans. Mundoo *likes* Wardley. He trusts him. And so do I. He must be king." *And he will grow to love me as I desire. He has to.*

Cheshire remained silent as they walked, finally arriving at the bright green lawn. Dozens of Cards labored in the waning light, fixing the landscape, polishing the statues, and removing the broken remnants of war. Dinah was proud to see progress made so quickly. Soon, the palace would shine again.

"Please continue with the next order of business, Cheshire."

He stared at her for a moment before his sly face twisted up in a smile, the newly grown beard on his chin making his face even more catlike than before. "Your Majesty, there is the question of what we should do with the king's body and head. Shall he be buried in your family tomb inside the palace? Or should we just burn him and throw out the remains with the filth from the day's chamber pots?" He gave a low chuckle, unnerving Dinah.

They stopped walking to let a few peacocks and flamingos strut past. Dinah recognized Vittiore's white peacock, Gryphon.

"Do we have his Heartsword?"

"Yes."

Dinah closed her eyes for a moment. "Build a small stone mount inside of the castle to hold the Heartsword. Have a smith engrave his name upon the sword. His ashes can be sealed inside the stone, but make the stone no higher than waist level. No one will look up to him."

Cheshire pulled a small scrap of paper from his pocket and scribbled upon it. "I will see to that this evening. As for the monument for your brother . . ."

Dinah turned to face him. "Charles should be in the gardens just outside his window. He should be able to see the stars from where he rests. Hire our best stoneworker to create something that Charles would love. I would like no penny spared for where he is laid, is that understood?"

Dinah blinked back a few tears and continued walking. Cheshire laid a hand on her shoulder. "Do you miss him?"

Dinah swallowed the longing in her throat. "I grieve him now even more than I did the day after his murder."

"Why?"

"Because I was running for my life, surviving. I didn't have time to grieve. But now that I am in this palace again, without him, it feels so empty, the wound so fresh. Without Charles, I am lost here."

She didn't mention to Cheshire that every night she had taken to wandering through the castle, with Ki-ershan following silently behind, and that she always ended up in the same place—Charles's empty room, staring up at the window that sent him into that dead, still night.

She dropped her voice to a whisper. "I miss him so much."

Cheshire smiled at her. "It will pass. Your brother was a damaged creature, and perhaps it is better for your rule to be untethered by such needy madness. He was not fit for rule, nor fit to share the blood of the queen."

Dinah stared up at him, aghast. "My father or not, you may never speak such things again! Charles was my brother, and his death will haunt me until the day I die." Her eyes cloudy, she stared unwaveringly at the setting sun. "The King of Hearts murdered him to frame me, and the guilt suffocates me from dawn until dusk. Do not presume that my life is easier without him."

A flush rose on Cheshire's cheeks as he bowed low

before Dinah. "Dinah, my queen, I didn't mean to offend, I only meant—"

"I know what you meant. Please, let's just continue on. I am eager to see the process of rebuilding my palace and army."

They walked and talked together, father and daughter. As the sun dipped in the sky, Dinah could hardly imagine darkness returning.

But come it did, from a most familiar place.

Thirteen

Days later, Dinah awoke in the middle of the night, convinced there was someone in her room. She sat up with a gasp, her hands moving to find the dagger underneath her pillow. She pushed herself up from the bed, her heart pounding wildly. She looked around her dark chambers frantically, the dagger poised to fling. There was no one in the room. Dinah clutched her chest, willing her heart to stop galloping. *She was safe. There was no one here.* She had been dreaming—something dark and twisted, something she barely remembered.

Dinah's breathing returned to normal as she watched Ki-ershan's shadow pacing just outside the door. If Ki-ershan wasn't leaping into action, then she knew there was no one in the room. Whatever had awakened her so suddenly was gone. Harris's loud snores echoed through the room, the low barrier between their chambers hardly enough to hold back the sound.

Dinah fell back into her bed with a long exhale of relief, gently tucking the dagger under her pillow. She closed her eyes and attempted to will unconsciousness back, but it wouldn't come. Sleep did not come easily to her, not even in this same bed, a bed that she had fantasized about when sleeping on the floor of the Twisted Wood. Now it was too soft, too filled with pillows and furs and feather blankets. It was suffocating in its loving embrace.

Dinah lay awake for another hour before she silently crept out of bed and washed her face in the silver basin near her swan-shaped tub. Reaching over the basin, she pulled on a black dressing gown. The inside swath that ran down the center of the garment was sewn with dozens of white and black squares, made to look like a chessboard. Her short hair was tangled and messy, and for a moment Dinah regretted cutting off her long, lovely black braid. She ruffled her hair in the mirror and jumped when she saw two glowing blue eyes reflected behind her.

"Ki-ershan! You scared me."

He was almost invisible in the darkness. "You are awake, so I must be. Will we be walking the palace again tonight?"

Dinah nodded. "I think so. I'm sorry. You should try to get some sleep."

He laughed. "I will do no such thing."

Dinah smiled. "I knew you would say that. I feel bad denying you sleep. Something woke me; I'm not sure what it was." Her voice faltered. The longer she was awake, the more she was convinced that it wasn't some *thing* that had woken her, but rather a *feeling*, a gnawing, mournful feeling in the pit of her stomach. It was the same feeling she'd had in the nights before she had awakened with a stranger's hand over her mouth. *A secret was passing through the palace.*

Ki-ershan checked the hallway first, strapping his sword across his back, then followed dutifully behind Dinah as she made her way through the dark corridors and hidden passages of Wonderland Palace. As they paced the sleeping palace, a growing sense of anxiety flooded Dinah's senses. Her bare feet slapped against the stone floor, faster and faster. It occurred to her that she was looking for something.

They had wandered for an hour when she decided to take a small detour.

Many of the Royal Apartments had secret exits and entrances, and the king's treasure—*now her treasure*, she mused—was scattered throughout the palace, hidden away in these secret rooms to keep it safe. It seemed like a good place to start. She tried door after door. Ki-ershan hurried along beside her, his muscles tensed, waiting for someone to leap out from these cobweb-covered corners.

They ducked under a table in the servants' kitchen and pushed open a tiny door, something Dinah had done several times as a child. After crawling through it, they stepped out into a long hallway, forgotten for the last ten years. Dinah passed several beat-up doors, each carved with a symbol of the Cards. These were the rooms where her father had met his mistresses. There was nothing of worth here. She passed the door marked with a Spade symbol, the Club, another door with a small heart carved around the keyhole, the Diamond carving. . . . These unassuming entrances were purposely designed to be forgettable. They were not the sort of doors that drew notice, as they were hidden dozens of twists and turns away from the day-to-day activity of the palace. The darkness that gnawed at her chest pressed hard against her.

Dinah walked past the doors and continued down the hallway. This was silly, she told herself. It was time to return to bed. She had turned to go when she heard something. A breath. A sigh. She spun around.

Without warning, there was a strange whiff of air as something ethereal, clothed in white, fluttered out of the darkness toward Dinah's face. Dinah silently leaped back, ducking her head as talons brushed the tips of her hair. Her face was gently bathed in long white feathers. The giant bird flapped to a stop and turned with a loud squawk.

The bird that had scared her so was Vittiore's white pea-cock, Gryphon. In fact, Dinah rarely saw Vittiore without Gryphon these days. When she walked, she cradled him so lovingly, as if he were her child. It hurt Dinah's heart to see it. The queen turned back to the wooden doors. She walked to the smallest one, carved with a rough heart.

Ki-ershan shook his head as he reached out and rested his fingers on Dinah's wrist.

"We should return to your chambers."

Dinah's eyes went wide with rage. The white peacock watched her silently, his head cocked to the side.

She looked at her bodyguard before quietly turning the door handle. It wasn't locked and they entered without a sound. The room smelled of heat—of skin and sweat and wanton perfume—and the scents mixed together assaulted her nostrils. There was only one small window in the entire room. Linens and clothing were strewn about the room, which was dimly lit by a dozen low candles and the stars outside. The flames flickered and leaped as Dinah inched silently toward the bed. When she reached it, she stood perfectly still, letting the black rage consume her from within.

Wardley and Vittiore lay face to face, their eyes closed in deepest slumber. Wardley's hair was pressed up against his forehead, the curls that Dinah loved damp and messy across his brow. His nose was inches from Vittiore's, his hand clasped lovingly over her cheek, as if he had fallen asleep caressing her face with his thumb. His chest, scarred and bruised like Dinah's, was bare and shining in the flickering light. One of Vittiore's arms was wrapped around his waist, the other pressed against his chest, her hand splayed over his heart. Her long white leg rested easily on his hip. She slept in the thinnest of gowns, the sheer blue fabric barely concealing her very naked body. Her tiny peach breasts heaved and fell with each deep breath. Wardley's other arm was wrapped beneath her, cradling her against him, their hips and legs entwined. The bed was bare except for their sweaty forms, all the linens stripped away by their lovemaking and crumpled up at the side of the bed.

Dinah stared down at their faces, so close that they breathed with one breath. The look on their faces was something she had never seen, not ever in all her years. *Perfect happiness.* Overwhelming sacredness, blissful contentment, ecstasy, and hope all blended in the faces of these two people, so deeply at peace that they did not stir as Dinah hovered over them. She had never known that happiness, and now she never would.

The rage she had kept at bay for so long, that seductive

fury, ripped its way out of her heart. It rose up from her chest, an anger as unstoppable as a tidal wave. Her fingers pulsed with it, the roots of her hair quivered with passion. Dinah's body began to shake, and then her vision tunneled. The candles and the walls faded away, and there was only her—*the queen!*—and the sleeping lovers, clinging to each other as if it was the end of the world. It was the end of her world.

Dinah moved faster than she ever had, with a strength that came from *somewhere else* pulsing through her muscles. Dinah grabbed a handful of Vittiore's thick golden hair and flung her out of bed. Vittiore weighed barely more than a feather. She bounced off a dresser before she really understood what was happening. Dinah leaned over her, her devastated ebony eyes full of rage, her mouth twisted in a violent smile. Vittiore wiped her eyes, confused, and then began crying, her hand held out in front of her.

"Oh Dinah, please! I'm sorry! Please, Your Majesty, let me explain! You don't understand!"

"I do understand," said Dinah calmly. She grabbed Vittiore's hair once again and began dragging her toward the door. Wardley, now wide awake, leaped from the bed.

"Dinah! Stop! What are you doing? Don't touch her!"

Dinah glanced at Wardley with dead eyes before picking up his sword where it lay forgotten beside the bed. She turned it over in the light, watching the flickering candles reflecting across the clean blade.

"Restrain him."

Ki-ershan stared back at her, utterly confused.

"I said, restrain him," she ordered, her voice flat and emotionless.

"No!" Wardley leaped across the room as Ki-ershan stared at Dinah. The Knave of Hearts twisted around and grabbed Ki-ershan's sword from his back. He lunged for Dinah. *The fool*, thought Dinah with a smile. Ki-ershan pounced on Wardley, whose hysterical voice bounced off the walls.

"Put the sword down. Don't do this! This isn't you! Please, gods, please!" Wardley was screaming at the top of his lungs now, his wrenching cries falling on deaf ears.

Ki-ershan struggled to regain control of the sword. Everything was happening so fast, but Dinah saw only

Vittiore. The girl who had stolen her crown, and now her future. Wardley's voice grew louder.

"Please! Dinah, stop! You are my friend. Please don't do this."

He brought the sword down toward Ki-ershan, who nimbly leaped out of the way. Dinah threw Vittiore down on the floor before her, one hand still tangled up in her hair, and brought her other hand hard across the girl's face. Then she yanked Vittiore onto her knees. Moving quickly, Dinah lifted Wardley's sword and pressed it against Vittiore's porcelain neck. Wardley let out a bellow, his entire body straining against Ki-ershan's arms.

"No, please, don't hurt her! Kill me, take me! Dinah, do not do this! You are not your father!" His face contorted as he howled. "Allllliiiiicccceeeeee!"

Dinah had never heard that name. She smiled a sad smile at Vittiore.

"Do you love him, Vittiore?"

"My name is Alice," Vittiore whispered in return. The girl's blue eyes found Wardley, and Dinah felt like she had been plunged into icy water. Wardley and Alice stared at each other, a thousand unspoken truths passing between them. Then she looked up at Dinah. "And yes, I do love him. I have loved him always."

Dinah let go of Vittiore's hair. The girl remained perfectly still, her eyes trained on Wardley, who writhed and screamed as Ki-ershan wrestled the sword from his grasp. Dinah stood tall, her figure illuminated by the moonlight and candles, which seemed to flare up with her roiling madness. She was only her rage.

"Not as long as I have."

With both hands, she brought the sword down on the girl's neck in one swift motion. Blood splattered Dinah's face. Alice's head fell from her body, landing facedown atop the pile of silk sheets. Her body gave a few twitches and collapsed beside it.

"Alice!" Wardley let out a scream, its wrenching sound tearing her away from the fury for just a moment. His hysterical cries seemed to shake the castle. "Gods, no!"

He fell forward. Ki-ershan stepped back and let him hit the floor, but as soon as Wardley's knees touched, he twisted away from Ki-ershan and grabbed a silver dagger that lay on a dresser. Wardley launched himself at Dinah, the dagger held aloft in his hands. He was quick, but the Yurkei warrior was quicker. Ki-ershan grabbed a silver candlestick and brought it down against his head with a sickening crack. Wardley's dagger was mere inches from Dinah's neck.

Wardley collapsed, unconscious, in Dinah's arms. Dazed, she looked at him, at the wet tears on his face, and then down at her gown, which was soaked with blood. She blinked. There was blood on her hands, the floor. It was all around her. The boiling fury receded from her vision, but in its place was a whirling circle of inky black.

Ki-ershan caught her before she hit the floor. Wardley slipped out of her arms. His body slumped against Vittiore's headless form, his head nuzzled against the small of her back. Before Dinah lost consciousness, she heard Iu-Hora's voice in her head. *She had cut out the heart of the one she loved most.*

Fourteen

Dinah swam slowly up toward consciousness. Up, up, out of the void, to light and hushed voices. Up, out of violent dreams filled with unspeakable horrors and bleak futures. Up, toward Harris, who softly called to her.

"Dinah, Dinah . . ."

Dinah opened her eyes. She was back in her chambers, in her own bed. She looked down. A plain white nightgown, completely without blemish or adornment, covered her body. Dinah exhaled a sigh of relief and let her head fall back onto the goose-down pillow. It had been a dream, thank the gods, the most terrible dream. Her eyes closed again, reaching back for the deep sleep that had eluded her that night.

"Dinah."

With a start, she turned her head and opened her black eyes. Harris's face was next to hers, his chair pulled up next to the bed. He cradled her face gently in his wrinkled hands, his skin like thin paper. His face was tired and worn, and his eyes were bloodshot.

"Oh, Dinah, my child." He rested his hand on her forehead. "What have you done?"

Dinah slowly raised up her hands. Dried blood covered them, deeply caked in the cracks of her fingers, crusted in the valley of her wrist.

"No!" She clumsily pulled herself out of bed and ran to her mirror. The monster in her dreams stared back at her. Blood speckles covered her face. Her tangled hair was matted and damp with sweat. Dried blood streaked her arms. The soles of her feet were covered with it. She let out a shriek.

"Get it off, Harris! Get it off me!"

He simply stared at Dinah.

"Get it off me! I command it!" She was hysterical now

as she made her way to the tub, climbing in and fumbling with the long, swan-necked spout that dangled from the ceiling. "Please, Harris! Help me!"

Harris's gaze was unwavering. A hissing stream of water poured out of the spout and Dinah held it over her head, not bothering to take off her nightgown. The scalding water burned her skin, but the dried blood began to flake off and form rivulets that circled the drain. Sobbing, she grabbed a hedgehog skin and scrubbed her hands, feet, and face until her own skin began to crack and bleed. Again and again she raked the washskin over her hands, muttering, "No, no, no, oh gods, no . . ."

Finally, Harris walked over. He took the hedgehog skin from her and set it down beside the bath. "No amount of scrubbing," he said simply, "will take the blood off your hands."

Dinah pulled her nightgown off and watched it float on the surface of the water like a crimson ghost.

Harris turned off the water and wrapped a towel around her red form, so hot that wisps of steam curled from her shoulders. As Dinah shook and cried, he draped a loose purple dress over her and ran a brush through her hair. She stared blankly into the mirror.

"I killed her."

"Yes."

"Wardley loved her."

"Yes."

"Did you know?"

Harris rose and began setting up tea in the corner. She turned and looked at him, her eyes wide.

"Did you know?"

"I suspected. But I never knew."

"Why didn't you tell me?"

Harris eyed the bathtub and the red rim around the drain. "For this very reason. Because I knew your reaction would be one of rage. I knew of the fury that burns inside you, even when you were small. So like your father—"

"But he wasn't my father. I'm not supposed to be like him at all."

Harris's hands trembled as he put the lid on the teapot. "It's true, you are not his natural child, but you have inherited his nature, since he was the only father you've ever known." He set the tea down before her. "I prayed that you would not do this. Do you understand what you have done to Wardley?"

Dinah's hands shook as she buried her face in them. "No. Yes. Oh my gods, Vittiore . . . Wardley . . ." She let out a sob. "He'll never forgive me! He loved her. I saw his face. . . ."

The pain of that statement twisted inside her, a hard thorn of truth. *He loved her.* He had never loved Dinah, not in that way. She had been chasing a ghost through these hallways. Now she had killed his lover. Her sister. Faina Baker's daughter. A daughter and mother beheaded, an entire family wiped out by the line of Hearts.

Dinah ran out to the balcony and proceeded to empty the remnants of food in her stomach. She knelt on the hard marble, her face pressed against the cool stone. A door slammed in her chambers and she heard snippets of a heated exchange between Harris and Cheshire. Cheshire's pointed boots came into view.

"Your Majesty, I implore you to get off the floor. We have much to do today."

Dinah looked at him with disgust. "Do you not know what I have done?"

Cheshire wrapped his hand around her arm and yanked her to her feet. He turned her face to the sweeping view from her balcony. "What do you see, my queen?"

"Cheshire, I killed her. In cold blood, I killed her."

Her adviser and father shook his head. "What do you see?"

"I see nothing," she sobbed. "Land and roads."

He grabbed her face with his long fingers. "Then you obviously cannot see clearly. When I look out, I see a kingdom in desperate need of a leader. I see a kingdom that is open to being sacked by the Yurkei. I see a kingdom that needs its queen, so you had best get off that filthy floor and put on your crown and do your duty."

Dinah yanked back. "I killed her. I murdered her. Do you understand?" She let out a gasp of horror. "Oh gods, I cut off her head." She couldn't breathe.

Cheshire stroked his chin. "I am quite aware of your actions, considering that I was forced to clean up your mess."

"Clean up?"

He nodded. "Ki-ershan came and found me not long after you sent the whore to her maker. He carried you back to your chambers. At my instructions, he changed your nightgown and burned the other. After that, he laid you in your bed and I took care of the rest."

Dinah's eyes grew wide with fear. "Where is Wardley? What did you do to him?"

"Don't worry, I didn't touch a curly hair on his head. He's been thrown into the Black Towers for now, where he can consider his actions."

Dinah gasped. "The Black Towers? No, you must retrieve him at once. I must speak with him."

Cheshire's black eyes found hers before he gave her a pitying smile. "He will not speak with you. You beheaded the love of his life before his eyes. Do you really believe you will be able to simply apologize and make it right?"

Dinah's eyes flooded with tears. *She had lost him. Forever.*

"I will not have him in the Black Towers. Have him moved here, to a secure location inside the castle. Make sure he has no weapons or anything to harm himself with, not even a bedsheet. And make sure he is well fed and clothed."

Cheshire gave a slight bow, annoyed by her orders. "As you wish. Though please remember that he is a liability to us that we cannot afford."

Dinah gasped. "What are you saying?"

"I'm saying that you do not understand what the consequences would be if word got out that the Queen of Hearts was a bloodthirsty murderer like the former King of Hearts. Your kingdom would fall. Mundoo would bring the Yurkei back and burn the city."

"He wouldn't. . . ."

"He would, and he could. If he finds out about this, he will turn his warriors around and they will ride straight back here, relieve you of your throne, and throw you in an empty grave. Mundoo can never know. We have no men to defend this city from an attack. You must destroy all the evidence of last night."

Dinah looked around. "Where is Ki-ershan?" Her voice rose. "Where is he?"

"Ki-ershan has been persuaded to keep his mouth shut. He is loyal to you, though I think he wonders why. He is resting now but will be back on your guard by nightfall."

Though she looked out onto the steady stones of the palace, Dinah could feel everything around her collapsing. Inside, her heart faded and shrank into itself. It was becoming a black, dead thing.

"Please leave me."

Cheshire hesitantly placed a hand on her shoulder. "Don't let guilt overcome you. You did what needed to be done. Vittiore—Alice—was a traitor, and by taking Wardley, she took something that belonged to the queen. Her death will make things much easier for all of us in the long run. Have no regrets, my daughter. The situation has been wiped clean. No one will ever know."

Dinah was flustered. "But . . . what will we tell the kingdom about Vittiore? They loved her."

"I have already set rumors in motion that she requested to be sent as an ambassador to Ierladia and that she left this morning. You know, it was too hard to see you on the throne here, and she didn't want to serve as a lady-in-waiting, and so on. A tragedy will befall her on the road. Pirates or robbers, I haven't decided yet."

Dinah narrowed her eyes as she stared at Cheshire in amazement. Of all the wonders she had seen in Wonderland, the mind of this devious man was by far the most impressive—and dangerous—one. Overnight, her crime had disappeared, though she doubted the scars she had left on Wardley would ever fade. Every time she blinked she saw Vittiore's golden curls, soaked with blood, and heard Wardley's screams of agony. Those screams would never leave her.

"What of her body?"

"It has been disposed of."

Dinah shuddered. "I am not in the mood for guessing games, Cheshire. What of her body?"

Cheshire's direct gaze pierced her flesh. "Burned. The ashes were scattered outside the palace. It is as if she never existed."

"That is . . ." Dinah searched for the word. Cheshire answered her before she could grasp it.

"That is the reality of being queen. You can make people disappear. The kingdom hinges on your actions, and therefore when the wheel needs to be turned in your favor, it will be. Now, on to other business . . ."

Dinah smacked his teacup and sent it shattering to the floor. "Other business? Other business? I murdered her! I killed her, with my own hands."

"You have killed many with your own hands, or have you forgotten the battle? Or even before that? What about the Heart Cards that you slew as you fled the castle? Faina Baker, who died because of you? Or the Yurkei warriors that Morte killed? The King of Hearts? How many, Dinah, have you killed? Your hands are hardly clean."

"Those were different."

"How so? Most of those people you killed to get your crown. War is a brutal act, and many innocents die in the cross fire. Vittiore stood between you and your future happiness with Wardley. You long to crown him king, gods know why, and she had manipulated his affections. There will always be bodies that litter your road to power. Every ruler has secrets."

"I did not want to start my rule with secrets. I don't want to be like him."

Cheshire stroked his beard. "Take heart that you are more like me than him. So, shall we lie in bed and cry for days about it? Or will you rise and rule? Today is just another day, my queen."

Dinah was staring at her hands again, at the half-moons of dried blood stuck underneath her fingernails.

"Leave me alone."

"Your Majesty."

"Get out!" she screamed.

Cheshire's eyes clouded over with disappointment, and he stalked toward the door. At the last moment, he whirled around. "Don't forget, she was nothing more than a fisherman's daughter from the Western Slope. In her heart, Vittiore was a *peasant*. A very pretty, poor little peasant named Alice. Her life is worth *nothing* compared to your crown, one that many of us have worked hard to get upon your stubborn head."

The heavy door slammed behind him, and for the first time in a very long time, Dinah was completely alone.

♥

Days passed in darkness. Dinah drew the shades and rarely strayed from her bed. Harris tried to coax her to move and to bathe, but she was haunted by her memories. Wardley's screams. The feel of the blade as it cut through Alice's neck. The finality in her eyes when she stared at Dinah. The way she and Wardley had been lying, so tangled up in each other. The musky smell of their passion that lingered in the air like smoke. Her name, Alice, so sweet and lovely, so fitting for the girl. Vittiore had been nothing more than a grand title bestowed by the King of Hearts, who found "Alice" to be simple and plain, unbefitting a queen. Dinah's dreams were filled with her, and she was vaguely aware that Alice would occupy each dream she ever dreamed again.

Ki-ershan returned, but his love for Dinah had obviously changed. He was distant—still her protector, but no longer her friend. He did not speak unless spoken to and soon faded into the very walls he stood against.

Harris counseled her, talked with her, prayed with her. But even his patience had a limit, and Dinah was frequently left alone with her thoughts. Alice drifted around her like a ghost, and Dinah became convinced that she was being haunted. She frequently found herself sitting up at night, shocked out of sleep by a malicious presence.

"Who's there?" Dinah would wave the candle around

her room. "Alice? Is that you?"

But the room never revealed anyone, and Dinah would lie back in bed, soaked with sweat, delirious, and very afraid. She ate only to live but not to enjoy. She took to drinking bottles of wine in the evening to help bring on sleep, but found herself visited by more and more terrors the emptier the bottle became. Everywhere, she saw the people she had killed. Men on the battlefield. The Heart Cards. Faina. Alice.

Dinah became convinced that nothing would ever change and she would die here alone, a bitter and defeated queen. She'd be loved by no one, as guilty as the King of Hearts, and never be the leader she was born to become.

Through her waking hours she heard Iu-Hora's words echoing in her head like a chorus: *You will cut out the heart of the one you love most.* So she had. And in the process, she had become mad. Mad like her brother, the Mad Hatter. The Mad Queen of Hearts, holed up in her palace.

Dinah was lying motionless in her bed when Sir Gorrann kicked down the door to her bedroom, letting in painfully bright streams of light.

"Get up." He yanked back her curtains and opened the doors to the balcony, letting in the early autumn breeze.

"Go away."

"Yeh stink like hell. Come on." He roughly tugged Dinah out of bed before shoving her toward the bath. "Here's what going to happen. Yer going to take a bath, put on yer clothes and yer crown, and then yeh are going to come with me to the council meeting."

"I—I can't," stammered Dinah. "You don't know what I did."

"I do know. Harris told me yer a murderous bitch, that's for sure! But yer also my queen, and it's time to rule." He stood before her closet, bewildered. "My gods. Which of these frocks does a queen wear? How about this nice, eh, peachy one? This is peach, right?"

"Black, red, or white," answered Dinah glumly. Any other colors would remind her of Alice, always.

He flung a deep-cranberry gown onto her dresser. Dinah looked away from it. The color reminded her of blood, of a head rolling on the floor. "Get out of my room."

"Not a chance. Yer going to get dressed and go to

council, and then yer going to rule yer kingdom. Otherwise Cheshire is going to take over; in fact, he already has. He's talking about imprisoning all the king's former advisers. . . ."

Dinah lifted her head. "What?"

"Yes, he's saying that they couldn't possibly be loyal to you, and so we should throw them into the Black Towers. . . ."

Dinah stood. "I will never throw anyone else into the Black Towers. And I appointed those men to my council. He has no right to remove them."

"Yes, well, yer words mean very little to Cheshire. And to be honest, since yeh can't be bothered to oversee yer kingdom, then he might as well."

"But without those advisers, we might not have the support of the court. And without the support of the court, we could be vulnerable to a rebellion. Not that a rebellion of clucking ladies in expensive dresses couldn't be easily quashed, but still—why would he want that? Why would he want to divide the council?"

Sir Gorrann grumbled, "These questions are why yeh should get dressed."

Dinah did. She washed and put on her makeup, something that Vittiore—no, Alice—normally did. Sir Gorrann placed the crown on her head, and Dinah stared back at herself in the mirror.

"I don't deserve it," she said quietly.

Sir Gorrann let his hand linger on her back. "Nope, yeh don't. Not after what yeh did. But maybe now yeh can earn it. Yeh'll have to start at the beginning, make yerself new."

"I will," she whispered.

She glanced at Ki-ershan, who stood silently beside her. "I will, I promise."

He stared back at her with his harsh blue eyes. Then he gave her a half nod.

Sir Gorrann clapped her on the back. "That's my girl. Now come, we need to hurry to the council."

They walked quickly through the palace halls and Dinah noticed that the servants smiled when they saw her in the hallways. A Card they passed bowed before her. "Your Majesty, I am so glad to see you up and well."

Dinah thanked him and continued on her way, then

paused. "Wait!" she called to him.

The Card, a young man she recognized, jumped and bowed again. "Your Majesty."

"Derwin! Derwin Fergal."

"My lady."

Dinah paused for a moment, weighing her options. Derwin had betrayed his king and helped her take the palace. She could trust him.

"Please take a message to Wardley. He is ill, so shove it underneath the door. Write that he is to meet me by the Julla Tree tomorrow, at sunset. Do not speak of this to anyone else, do you understand?"

The Card nodded, and Dinah knew he would never tell anyone. Not Derwin, so eager for promotion.

He bowed at the waist. "Of course, my queen."

"And Fergal?"

"Yes, Your Majesty?"

"Your arrow shot true."

He grinned.

Dinah and Sir Gorrann continued down the hall

to meet with the council. She had neglected to address the needs of her domain—she had almost abandoned her kingdom.

She allowed herself a fleeting moment of fantasy. Perhaps if she showed Wardley she could be a good queen, if she could rule with grace, then maybe he could forgive her one day.

In her heart, she knew it would not be so.

Q
♥

Fifteen

Dinah's hands were damp with sweat as she wrung them together, harder and harder, until her skin blistered. She paced back and forth before the Julla Tree. She had never been this nervous, not even before the battle when she rode out to an almost certain death, her heart hammering with fury and ecstasy. Now, her heart was slow, its dull beats echoing inside her chest.

She wore a simple black dress, her short hair pulled back in a low bun. Her dazzling crown rested on a mossy rock nearby, as did Ki-ershan, who sat patient and silent, his eyes taking in the ever-darkening sky. The stars lined up in a giant whorl tonight, the corners of the swirling creation touching just above the Western Slope. Behind Ki-ershan, she knew, sat a loaded bow and arrow. It was just a precaution.

As she waited, there was a crack of light in the darkness, followed by angry mumbling of men. Sir Gorrann appeared along with two Spades, each of whom walked beside a man whose hands were bound in front of him in chains. *Wardley.* The last few weeks had changed him greatly. He was painfully thin and his muscles were softer, looser. The brown curls that Dinah so loved were slick with grease and dirt, and he wore nothing more than a worn pair of wool pants. Dinah was furious.

"I told Cheshire to move him from the Black Towers!"

"He did, Your Majesty," answered Sir Gorrann. "Wardley's been given a room with clean clothing and more than enough food. He just refuses to eat or bathe or change."

Wardley let out a wicked cackle. Dinah winced as he came closer. The shadow of a bruise covered the top of his forehead all the way down to his left eye. Dark circles, the color of ripe plums, stretched below his eyes to his pale and sunken cheeks. His eyes were hollow and dead, and he stared at Dinah with complete indifference.

"Leave us, please," she ordered.

Sir Gorrann and the Spades walked away, leaving Wardley standing just a few feet from the new queen. Dinah pulled a key from her pocket and walked over to him.

"Here, they are surely hurting your wrists."

Wardley yanked back, trembling.

"Don't touch me! Don't come near me, you, you . . . monster!" He fell back over one of the Julla's roots and scrambled into a crouched position near the ground. "Please go away. Leave my chains be. Otherwise, I will strangle you where you stand."

His words pierced her heart, and she felt her eyes sting with hot tears. She had been expecting his raw hatred, but seeing it before her was like sinking into dark, seething waters. Slowly, she sat down beside him, making sure to put some room between them.

"Wardley . . . I'm so sorry for what I did to Alice."

"Don't say her name. You never get to say her name, not ever again!"

He struggled to control the pain on his face. Dinah studied him, her love, so lost in grief that he could barely look at her.

"I lost control. I didn't know what was happening."

"You cut off the head of the woman I loved. She was the light in my life, and you cut off her head. Every time I close my eyes, I see her blood. . . ."

Dinah reached for his face. "Me too. I dream of her every night."

Wardley spat at her. "You would be so lucky to dream of her. My dreams are filled with nothing but unending sorrow. Caused by you, Dinah. She was everything I lived for, everything to me—"

"I don't want to hear that," replied Dinah quietly.

Wardley smiled. "And yet you will. You will look at me and you will listen to our story, so that you can know what you took from me. You will hear how deeply I loved her."

Dinah focused on him, the circling stars tracing light on his chin. He was as lovely to her as the sun, and she would never have him, not ever. Listening to his words would be akin to torture, and yet, she had no choice. This was the beginning of a lifetime of penance. She nodded. "All right."

"I met Alice even before you did. Alice in Wonderland, my heart, my life. The first time I saw her, I was walking through the palace, searching for some rare bird that I wanted to catch and show you. She was walking with your father—it was that same day that your father announced her to the court. She walked by me, this tiny creature, delicate and light and lovely. Her eyes . . ." He shook his head, his own eyes full of tears. "They were so blue, so sad. Looking at her was like being blinded by light. I surrendered immediately to her gaze, to the fact that I would be her slave forever. I desired to run my fingers through her golden hair, trace my lips over her pale skin. Seeing Alice ignited something in me that I had never even known, a passion, a need, a love. She was like a dream, only she was *my* dream. I watched as your father introduced her to you later that day, and I immediately saw in your eyes such fierce hatred."

He shuddered.

"Your eyes chilled me. At the time, I thought you were justified, but now I know the truth: you were insanely jealous of her, of the imagined love that you assumed the King of Hearts lavished on her. She gave you even more reason to feel isolated and betrayed. She represented so many things that you would never be: innocent, loved. My darling little Alice, so quiet and scared. She never had to work for people to love her like you did. She was kind, and saw beauty in all things and all people."

Wardley took a deep breath, choking on a sob.

"And gods, did I love her. I began bringing her gifts, leaving them at her door. I wrote her letters, and she wrote me back, sharing stories of the sea, fairy tales of flying boys, talking animals, and wondrous creatures of the deep. My letters were confessions of love. Hers were stories, though her affection for me grew in each stroke of her pen. She was lonely. The King of Hearts treated her terribly, as did Cheshire. The king forced her to become what he wanted in a daughter—someone who would someday be a meek queen, silent and content to let her father do the ruling. He was sculpting her into everything you could and would never be.

"You and I, we went into the Black Towers like foolish children on a treasure hunt, and for that the king beheaded Faina, her mother. I will never forgive myself for causing her that pain. After that, Alice told me the truth—where she was from, her real name, and the vague inkling that the king was planning something sinister. She tried, so many times, to befriend you, and you—you stubborn, wicked girl—would have none of it. She could have been a sister, an ally, and you made her your enemy, though she never viewed you that way."

Dinah could take no more. Hearing of their love was like a black root twisting into her brain, each curl penetrating into her deepest secrets and desires. He had lied to her. So many lies, she couldn't even trace where they began. Everything she believed about her life had been untrue, and now the tapestry of her existence was nothing more than a pile of string. All those imagined passions between her and Wardley—they were nothing now. Anger rose inside her. Dinah had told herself to be patient, to listen, but she felt a pressing and silly need to defend herself. *Wardley needed to know.*

"She stole my crown. She took the crown made for me and wore it upon her head. She was a stranger, and you knew it!"

Wardley leaped to his feet with a roar, the chains rattling in front of him.

"She never wore your crown! She never wanted the crown, never! All she longed for was a quiet life by the sea— with me!"

He took a deep breath, and it seemed to Dinah that he hadn't taken one in a while. A smile crept over his face and he closed his eyes.

"We began meeting, in secret. It was like coming home, only my home was her hair—which smelled like salt water and honey. With her, I was completely at rest. Completely myself. Whenever we could manage it, we would stay together until the sun rose in the west, tangled together, in sweat and tenderness. In love."

A sharp corkscrew was turning into Dinah's chest now, silver and hard. She ached with longing for this to be her story, but it wasn't.

"I loved her more than I've ever loved anything, or anyone. It was as if my soul had taken residence in her body. That day, when you found Charles thrown out the window, Vittiore woke me from slumber and told me that the king was in a fury, telling people that you killed the prince. I ran to the stables to meet you—"

"And you sent me off. Into the Twisted Wood, alone."

"Dinah, I couldn't leave her! I knew you didn't kill Charles, but if the King of Hearts was willing to kill his own son, what would he do to Vittiore—to my Alice? I couldn't leave her behind, defenseless. But as you rode away, as I lay bleeding on the stable floor, a part of me was ripped away. My loyalty was torn. I felt I had done something shameful."

His brown eyes met hers, and Dinah's guilt was overwhelming as she saw the pain in them. The pain she had caused with the single stroke of a sword. A pain that she could see now would never be forgiven.

"You were my best friend, *like a sister*. I knew that you wanted me to be more, but since the day I saw Alice, I have never been able to even see another woman. Dinah, I was destroyed when you left. I kept imagining you lost, alone in the Twisted Wood. I stopped sleeping. My nights were filled with the joy of Alice's lips, but my days were torturous, thinking I'd betrayed you, my queen. When Cheshire approached me with a plan to convince the Spades to join your side, I leaped at the chance. I should never have sent you out on your own, without my protection."

His eyes narrowed.

"Of course, now I would have fed you to that white bear myself. Alice told me to go. She promised she would wait for me."

His mouth trembled with anger. Tears dripped down his cheek as he screamed in her face.

"Do you understand? I left her for you! We both knew that we couldn't stay together once you became queen, and I became king, but I could no more avoid her than I could stop breathing. I love . . . loved her. Then you came that night. . . ."

The wind howled, and the trees of the Twisted Wood answered with a low moan, a sound that Dinah knew well. She turned for just a moment. Wardley moved swiftly, pushing his chained wrists out from his body and leaping forward, knocking her to the ground. The man she loved was on top of her now, the irons of his chains pulled tight against her bare neck. Dinah choked as she stared up at him.

"You killed her . . . the woman I loved! You cut off her head because you couldn't have me, and couldn't love me, even though there are thousands of men in Wonderland who would have you!"

Dinah began to struggle, her hands reaching for his face.

"You burned her body! You burned her eyes, her curls, my Alice! Now I can't even say good-bye. You took everything from me!"

His tears dripped on her face, and Dinah stopped struggling. She dropped her arms to the ground and lifted her neck.

"Do it," she coughed, barely able to speak. "Do it. I deserve it."

She would rather die than face the pain she had caused him. The world around her began to fade into spotty blackness as the chain pressed harder against her throat.

Wardley was looking down at her now, his face contorted with pain as he pushed the life out of his best friend. Finally, with a loud cry, he sat back and jerked her up to a sitting position, the chains still around her neck. Ki-ershan stood silently nearby. Ki-ershan had let this happen to her, because she needed it. Wardley needed it. The love of her life began sobbing into his open hands.

"Why? Why did you do this to me? You were my best

friend. I would have gladly died for you."

Dinah rolled over and put her head against his knees.

"I love you, Wardley," she whispered. "I wish I could say more, but . . . I love you. I'm so sorry. I know you will never forgive me, but know that I will live with the guilt over the pain I caused you both for the rest of my life."

Wardley brought his elbow across her nose, and Dinah felt blood begin to run down her face as her nose went numb. Hatred contorted his face as he hissed damning words at her.

"You are just like your fathers. Both of them. You are the *worst* of both of them. I see you now for who you really are."

Dinah wiped the blood dripping from her face onto her sleeve and stood shakily as sobs broke loose from her throat.

"It is not who I will be! What do you desire? What do you want from me? Freedom? Money? Take Corning tonight, and I'll fill your purse with gold. Go to Hu-Yuhar, or to the Western Slope. Live out her dream. Just go!"

Wardley shook his head and glanced up at the palace, glowing now from the hundreds of burning torches that lit its many halls.

"This is where I loved her. This is where I knew her. I

can be in no other place. Besides, I want you to see my face *every day*. I want you to see what your fury wrought."

Dinah's heart, it seemed, gave one final thump and grew silent.

"Give me your chains," she said quietly. Her hands shaking, she unlocked the iron shackles, watching as they fell into the grass.

Wardley looked again at Dinah, his eyes darkened with exhaustion and hatred as he rubbed his wrists. "I might still decide to kill you, you know."

She nodded.

"I'm sorry for what I've done, Wardley. I will make it up to you, someday."

"You never can. She was the love of my life, Dinah, and you were my best friend. I have nothing left." He began limping away from her, toward the palace, but turned, offering yet another scornful, "I was wrong—you never deserved, and never will deserve, the crown on your head."

Dinah let a wave of dizziness wash over her in the darkness, and her stomach turned over. Something about the crown . . .

"Wardley! Wait!"

He turned around again, this time defeated and sad.

Dinah narrowed her eyes, her forehead crinkled in thought. "What did you mean, when you said she never wore my crown?"

"What?"

"You said she never wore my crown. But she was crowned queen, was she not?"

Wardley walked over to the rock where Dinah had placed her crown and picked it up, turning it over in his hands. The Mad Hatter's elaborately crafted crown of diamonds sent thousands of tiny lights across his pained face.

"Alice never wore this crown. I'd never even seen it before your coronation. Hers was small, and blue. Perfectly lovely. Just like her."

He let the crown drop from his hands, and it bounced off the rock and landed in a bed of wild thistle with a heavy thud. Wardley started walking away, the soft whisper of his voice dancing on the wind. "I wish you had died on the battlefield. It's what I wish every day, when I wake up." Dinah let his words cut into her, a swift blade to the heart. Then she bent over and picked up her crown, her face puzzled as it reflected the moonlight.

♥

Back in her chambers, nursing the growing bruise creeping across her neck, Dinah pulled book after book down from the shelf. Harris came in, rubbing his eyes.

"Child, what are you searching for? It's quite late, and you haven't even been to bed."

Dinah barely looked up. "Harris, I'm glad you're awake. Help me find something."

"Let me get my spectacles."

After a few minutes of searching, Dinah found his glasses and together they pulled a giant, dusty book down from the shelf. *Wonderland: A History*. Dinah flipped it open.

"Does this have the list of traditions and ceremonies in it?"

"Why, yes!" Harris hopped from one foot to the other excitedly. "Are you fancying learning more about those things? A good queen should always know—"

"No. I'm not." Frustrated, Dinah shoved the book toward him. "I need to find the order for a coronation ceremony."

"Hmmm..." Harris licked his finger and paged through a thick index. "Ah, yes. Here. Oh, this is very interesting."

"Harris."

"Sorry. Here it is." He turned the book toward Dinah and pointed at an elaborate list of rules and practices. Dinah ran her finger down the worn pages, flipping to the next, and then the next.

"This is what I was looking for. Listen." She read aloud.

"'When a daughter takes the crown of Wonderland, she, by law, must wear the most extravagant crown in the kingdom. In most cases, the crown shall pass down from queen to queen, but only after the first queen's death or forfeiture of her rule. If ever a crown is made of superior size and glory, then the new crown shall crown the queen, with the former crown melted and turned into jewelry.'"

She looked at Harris with amazement.

"The crown!"

Harris sat down at the table, disappointment written on his face.

"I'm surprised that you did not know that already. Did you listen to nothing I taught you?"

"That's beside the point. At her coronation—what crown did Vittiore wear?"

Harris bit his lip and looked at the floor. "As you may remember, my queen, I was imprisoned in the Black Towers during the coronation. But I'm sure it was a wonderful event."

Dinah reached out and laid her palm across his hand. "Wardley said that Vittiore—Alice, whoever—did not wear this." She pointed to her own splendid diamond crown, resting on its designated lavender pillow. "In fact, Wardley said he had never seen it."

"And?"

"And why wouldn't the king give *this* crown to Vittiore? Or wear it himself even? No finer crown has ever been made in the history of Wonderland. The king took everything he ever desired, that was his nature, and so why wouldn't he take my crown and put it on *her* head? It would have been symbolic, fitting even. The king would do that, would he not?"

Harris's head was tilted. "Yes, he would. He was a man who loved to make examples of anyone who crossed him. Putting the crown your brother made for you on Vittiore's head would have brought him great pleasure. He was wicked that way."

"Exactly. So why didn't he? Why didn't Vittiore or the king wear this crown?"

There was a silence in Dinah's chambers. Ki-ershan sat awake on his cot, his chest rising and falling with silent breaths. Dinah looked down at the book, and back at Harris again, this time with wide eyes.

"Because the king didn't *know* about the crown. He never knew it existed."

Harris lowered his glasses.

"What does this mean to you, then? You look positively stunned. I don't understand."

Dinah began pacing back and forth in front of the table. "The night I found Charles, the crown he made for me was missing. I assumed that the king took it, since he had been there. But the king didn't have it. He didn't know about it."

"Which means?" Harris was looking concerned now, beads of sweat pooling on his forehead.

"Which means that someone else was in Charles's room that night. Someone who took the crown. I have to go. Right now."

"Dinah, it's the middle of the night. You can't go anywhere. You've had a very taxing day."

Dinah felt her sore neck, a fresh wave of guilt and shame washing over her. *Was she so like her fathers? Could she choose a different path? Was it too late?*

"I have to go. Ki-ershan?"

But Ki-ershan was already out of bed, strapping a bow and arrows to his back and tucking a dagger into his waistband.

"Where are you going?" Harris asked.

"Into town. No one can know I am gone. Do you understand? No one."

Harris bowed before her.

"I'll be back before first light. Hopefully." She kissed his ruddy cheek.

"Where are you going?" Harris asked again, looking worried, tapping his feet under the table.

"To find two lords."

With that, Dinah rushed out the door, a black cloak swirling after her, her Yurkei guard by her side.

Sixteen

Scurrying through the alleys like rats, Dinah and Ki-ershan made their way from the palace to the lower residences of the court. These small but distinguished houses bordered the sides of the palace, occasionally jutting out like crooked teeth.

The houses of the court were built so that the buildings connected with one another by use of tunnels, hallways, and hidden doors. One man's kitchen might back up to another man's bedroom, and walls were thin. They were a perfect little puzzle of gossip, drinking, and other scandalous activity, all of which kept the court very entertained.

Dinah and Ki-ershan ran through the darkness, hiding periodically in crevices and under stoops to avoid Cards or townspeople. After checking their surroundings, Dinah stepped up to a stone house, clustered against several others in the damp evening. She peered at the names posted above the door, written in a muddled scrawl. "Lord and Lady Geheim. That's so strange. . . ."

One door after another, they continued checking for the two names Dinah was looking for. She was vaguely familiar with which family resided in which homes—this from making endless rounds of teas and tarts with the ladies of the court—but the names she was looking for weren't here. They reached the end of the row, and Dinah stomped her feet with frustration on the immaculately manicured lawns.

"I was sure that they lived on this row. Sure of it . . ."

Ki-ershan stood silently beside her. She stopped for a moment and ran a hand over her chin, following a thread of memory that linked back to her carefree days of chasing Wardley through these alleys and streets. With a smile, she turned to Ki-ershan.

"Follow me."

Dinah circled back to the first house she had checked, the residence of Lord Geheim. His door was painted a lovely shade of lavender.

"Lift me?" she asked Ki-ershan. He gave her a doubtful look but did as she commanded. Teetering on his shoulders, Dinah peered closely at the sign overhead and brushed at it with her hand. Black charcoal covered her fingers. Frantically, she rubbed the sign with the cuff of her sleeve. *Lord Geheim* washed off cleanly, and beneath it, carved directly into the wood, was one of the names she was looking for— *Lord Delmont*.

"Yes," she whispered. "Put me down."

Dinah pulled up the hood of her cloak and pounded on the door. No one answered. She pounded again, this time with repeated thrusts, meant to scare whoever was inside. The door cracked open, and a tiny blond girl with her hair in ringlets opened the door. For a minute, Dinah's breath was sucked away. She didn't look anything like Alice, and yet, the blond curls still froze her in place.

"May I help you, ma'am?" the child asked shyly.

"What business do you have here?"

"I need to speak to Lord and Lady Geheim, if you please." Dinah smiled at the girl, who did not smile back.

The door shut in her face with a slam, and Dinah could hear raised voices inside. Lord Geheim eventually yanked open the door and glowered down at her, his wild white hair transparent in the moonlight. He squinted his eyes in the darkness.

"Vagrants! How dare you interrupt my night with my family. What business have you here, in the houses of the court?"

Dinah dropped her own voice to a whisper, hoping he would do the same.

"I need to speak with you, sir. May I come inside?"

"You may not! Get out of here, take your filth and go! Perhaps find a place to sleep, or maybe go whore yourself out to the Spades. I'm sure they could use some warm thighs to comfort them in their barracks."

He waved his hands as if she was a cat he was shooing away. Dinah stepped forward into the light and let her hood fall from her face.

"Do not come any closer, wretch, or—"

Dinah saw his eyes narrow in confusion and then widen. Geheim dropped to his knees.

"Oh gods, Your Majesty! I apologize. I did not realize it was you!"

Lady Geheim, standing behind her husband, dropped to the ground, followed by the towheaded child. The older man was stammering now.

"I have spoken ill to the queen. Gods have mercy. Your Majesty, please forgive me. Please do not take your anger out upon my family, I beg of you, not for my insolent tongue!"

Dinah walked into the house, Ki-ershan at her heels. It was elaborately decorated, filled with golden trinkets and chandeliers. Like most houses of the court, the family's wardrobe was in the center of the room, with candy-colored dresses and suits hung on a rotating pulley system. It was surrounded by high-backed chairs, so that the family could admire their belongings as they took their tea. Dinah spied one of her brother's hats hanging on a lower rung. She cleared her throat as she surveyed the trembling family.

"There is no need for such pleading apologies, though

I would ask you to have more sympathy for those less fortu-
nate than yourself. You never know who is knocking on your
door."

"You are correct, Your Majesty."

"You may rise. I am here to ask about Lord Delmont.
Where might he be found?"

Lord Geheim rose to his feet, though his eyes remained
glued to the ground.

"I'm sorry to be the one to have to share this with you,
my queen, but Lord Delmont is dead."

"And how did he come to be that way?"

Lady Geheim rose and stepped closer to Dinah. Dinah
had spoken with her many times in passing. The heavy
makeup she normally wore was washed cleanly from her
face, revealing a spry and lovely older woman, with friendly
crow's-feet creeping away from sad brown eyes. Her graying
hair fell gently away from her face.

"I am surprised that you have not heard, Your Majesty.
Lord Delmont and his family fell violently ill, victims of
some disease that lurked in their dinner. Doves, they had
that night. Within hours, the entire family was dead. All

here, in this house. The cook was executed by the king, and the dove coop burned to the ground." Her eyes welled with tears. "It was such a sadness. Lord Delmont was a kind man, who loved his family. I heard he had fallen into some debt, but that he was slowly repaying his debts and caring for his family."

She gave a sob. Dinah handed her a handkerchief from inside her cloak. Lord Geheim looked appalled that his wife would soil an item belonging to the queen, but the crying woman gladly wiped her eyes and nose with it.

"Lord Delmont had four children. Four boys, all in the prime of their youth, just like my Lyla. To think they died from boiled dove meat . . ." She dissolved into tears again.

Dinah hesitantly reached out and squeezed her shoulder. Ki-ershan raised his eyes to hers, and Dinah gave him a knowing look. Without warning, the little girl who had been watching them silently reached out to grab Ki-ershan's hand. He looked down at her curiously as she gazed up at him in amazement. Lord Geheim walked across the room swiftly and scooped up his daughter.

Ki-ershan winked at the girl as Lord Geheim returned

to the corner, holding his daughter protectively. Dinah thought about reprimanding him but decided against this fruitless effort. She turned back to the lady of the house.

"Was there anyone who Lord Delmont confided in? Anyone he was close to outside of his family?"

Geheim cleared his throat. "He was extremely close to Lord Sander, whose old residence was at the end of this row."

"Was?"

"Did you not hear? Lord Sander and his family died in the battle. They were slain."

"By?"

Lord Geheim shrugged, his eyes weary. "Does it matter? Lord Sander died on the battlefield, and his family was slain by a blade—probably Yurkei—while trying to barricade themselves in their home."

He collapsed on a chair in the living room, his daughter on his lap, all traces of nervousness wiped out by exhaustion.

"These are dark times for the court of Wonderland. Our lives were once full of dancing, tea and tarts, fashion and feasting. Now, life is a hardship we can hardly bear." Dinah looked at him with amazement. He was a wealthy man, living in a fine house with servants at his command. *Hardship?* She realized with a start just how naive the court was. They were nothing more than children who played at Wonderland Court. Lord Geheim continued, unaware of her skeptical eyes.

"I pray that your rule will bring the peace that we have so needed, even if it does come at a *cost*."

His eyes lingered on his daughter, who was still staring with fascination at Ki-ershan.

Dinah sighed. "Is there anything else you can tell me about either of those two lords? Anyone they were consorting with?"

"Not that I can think of, Your Majesty. I am sorry that I cannot be of more help."

Dinah stood and fiddled with her cloak strings. "Thank you for your time. I would ask that you speak of this to no one, not a word. Do you understand? Keep in mind that this is a matter of the crown, and speaking of it will carry a high cost."

Lord and Lady Geheim's faces paled. They understood what that meant.

"And might I suggest the next time you have visitors, offer them some tea—both of them."

On her way out, she patted the little girl on the head. The girl beamed up at her like she was the sun. Dinah paused.

"I think I would like Lyla to become one of my junior ladies-in-waiting. Please send her up to the palace early next week to begin training."

Lady Geheim gasped and put a hand over her heart. Then she gave a clumsy curtsy before sinking to the ground and gushing. "That is a great honor, Your Majesty. How can we ever thank you?"

"You can thank me by your silence."

Ki-ershan checked outside the door and then ushered Dinah through it. They had walked only a few steps before Lord Geheim ran out, his nightshirt blowing around his ankles.

"Wait! Your Majesty—I just remembered something that may be helpful. Lord Sander had an apprentice, a young boy. His name is Swete Thorndike. I think he lives in the baker's district."

Dinah's black eyes bore into his. "Thank you."

He bowed before her. "My queen."

Ki-ershan and Dinah swiftly made their way to the baker's district. It was hardly a district—more like a cluster of carts and a few bakeries. The houses were smaller here, but still pretty and quaint. Though it was very early in the predawn hours, the lights of the bakers' houses were ablaze with pink flames. The inhabitants were up early, baking bread for the day. The smell of warm yeast drifted up and through the lots, and Dinah's stomach gave a quiet grumble.

As they came around a corner, she spied a round woman stacking loaves of steaming bread onto a cart. The woman's heavy breasts swung forward in her tunic as she covered the loaves with a checkered blanket. Dinah and Ki-ershan approached and the woman slyly reached under her cart, probably looking for a weapon. Dinah pulled back her hood, revealing her black hair.

"We are not here to hurt you, madam. I am simply looking for the house of Thorndike."

The woman narrowed her eyes at Dinah, trying to put together where she had seen this woman before.

"I'm Ruby Thorndike. How can I help you?"

"Yes, I'm looking for your son, Swete."

The woman's eyes filled with tears. "Do you know where he is? Has he been found?"

Dinah shook her head. "No, I'm sorry. We are looking to speak with him regarding Lord Sander."

The woman slammed her hand on the cart, and a loaf of bread rolled off and bounced onto the ground. "Lord Sander," she hissed. "Don't speak to me of him! Coward that he is! He's responsible for everything."

Dinah gestured for the woman to sit on a stone bench near the cart and lowered herself beside her. The woman's eyes went wide when she recognized Dinah.

"Why, you're . . . you're the Rebel Queen!"

Dinah smiled kindly. "Just the queen now. But please continue."

"Yes, Your Majesty. As I was saying, Lord Sander and his highborn family took my son away. I was raising him to be a baker, like his father, who died when Swete was two. Raising him to love bread, just like his mother. There was flour on the boy's hands since the day he was born. But Swete wanted more. He wanted to be a member of the court—a ridiculous lot of useless birds though they are, even if their coins keep us from being cast out of Wonderland proper."

She leaned forward and continued pulling loaves out of the cart.

"Swete followed Lord Sander around, trying to learn everything he could and work his way up into his good graces. Lord Sander indulged him, teaching him how to make ale, how the lords and the ladies dressed. All nonsense, in my opinion. Yet he never invited him to join him at court, never gave the lad anything of value. My son was no more than a servant, a pet to amuse him!" She spat on the ground.

"One day Swete came home and he was mumbling, nervous, terrified. He clutched a package in his hands and kept glancing around nervously. Said that he had to hide something, said that Lord Sander had fallen in with someone unsavory. Sander owed a debt, a debt to someone *dangerous*. Swete feared for Lord Sander's life, and now I wonder if he feared for his own as well. That day he swore to me that he was never going back to Lord Sander. I didn't ask about the details—I was blinded, you see, happy to have my son back, so I didn't want to upset him. I asked him to show me what was in the package, and he said he couldn't. So I didn't ask again. That was almost a year ago." She wiped tears from her eyes.

"Things returned to normal. Then the Queen of Hearts—er, I mean you—rode on our fair city. Lord Sander died on the battlefield—a knife to the throat!—but we fared okay. Swete returned safely from outside the north wall, gods be good. Two days after the battle, we began making bread again. The Cards needed it. But a week later, my son went to bed, and the next morning, he was gone. His clothing and bags were still there, and his bed had been barely disturbed. All that was left of my son was a single drop of blood, left in the middle of his pillow. I looked for the package but couldn't find it. I have no proof. I have no son."

Dinah knew where the package was. She dropped her eyes as thoughts raced through her brain. "I'm sorry for your loss."

"Sorry? Why should you be sorry? Lord Sander should have been sorry for what he did to my son, my innocent boy. He wrapped him up in his shady dealings, and now I have no son, no husband, no family. I am glad for Lord Sander's death. I would dance on the man's grave."

Ruby Thorndike picked up the loaf of bread that had fallen to the ground, brushed it off, and placed it back on the cart. "I am sad for his family. His wife was a kind woman who took to Swete. But whoever Lord Sander got involved with took or murdered my son. I am sure of it."

Dinah turned away from the woman to hide her face. Her heart raced. The pieces were falling into place, but she wanted a quiet spot to think. The sun would be rising soon, and she needed to get back to the palace.

"We must go," she muttered. "Now."

Dinah nodded at Ki-ershan, who swiftly gave the woman a single heavy gold piece, equal to two years' wages. She gasped.

"I know that this cannot buy your son back. If I were you, I would take this money and head for one of the towns on the Western Slope. Start a new life. It is for your silence, and for your loss. Go now, and do not wait. Wonderland is no longer a safe place for you."

The woman's hands shook. "Thank you, Your Majesty! How can I hope to repay you?"

Dinah paused a moment and then plucked a loaf of warm bread from her cart.

"This will do nicely. Thank you."

Dinah walked away from the woman, who gazed after her with amazement.

As they ran back to the palace, Ki-ershan was obviously annoyed by her much slower pace, but it couldn't be helped. Dinah was overwhelmed. She felt as if the stars themselves were falling all around her, like she was back in the Sky Curtain. Everything around her plummeted to the ground, illuminating all the parts of her mind that had lain dormant for weeks. Her heart and chest, already bloody and raw from what she had done to Alice, felt like they were ripped open.

In this still night, all was so clear, but Dinah knew if she hesitated for even a moment, it would become cloudy again. Her mind reeled as she connected the pieces, and she began to see things take shape in the dark, things that she hadn't let herself ever consider before. She let out a long breath as her strong legs pumped underneath her. Ki-ershan's eyes glowed in the darkness. To anyone watching, the sight of the queen and a Yurkei warrior racing toward the palace would be strange indeed.

Dinah pulled the hood of her cloak back over her head. *There will come a day*, she thought, *when I will no longer have to sneak around. There will be no more whispered secrets, no more insistent fear and doubt.* Memories flooded her senses, and everything fell swiftly into place. *Charles, giving her the crown. Charles, his tiny body cradled in her arms. Lord Delmont, poisoned. Lord Sander, killed in battle. Swete, poor innocent Swete, who never knew what he held in his hands.* The swirling flurry of questions in her mind fell to the ground. Behind the confusion and doubt was only one person. One person who was probably already aware of what she was seeking. He was the key to her rule, to her crown, to her fate. He was always one step ahead of everyone.

Her father, the man in the purple cloak.

Cheshire.

Seventeen

The next night was void of stars, as if they knew what was about to transpire. Dinah's fingers shook in the cool night as she clutched a dagger marked with a purple amethyst, a gift from her father. She had thought like him, planned like him, and now she waited for him. This was Dinah's first time in the Spades' barracks, which were in the process of being completely torn down. And while she had supported the rebuilding of the Spades' residences, she had not fully understood *why* until now. Under the shadows of the Black Towers, the Spades' barracks were the equivalent of a shantytown. Stacked and cornered, each little stall pressed uncomfortably against the one before it, the barracks were more a prison than a home.

Inside was a maze in shades of black—black walls made with black wood. There were very few windows. Small tree roots of the Black Towers rose and fell all across the ground. The soil underneath her feet was grainy and soft at the same time, and quite hard to navigate without tripping. A feeling of hopelessness—a little sadness, a little madness—made the rooms feel even more dark and ominous. It was the same feeling that Dinah had experienced in the Black Towers, only diluted to make the place barely livable. *No wonder the Spades were so angry.* The Black Towers fed off their misery and then gave it back to them.

When Wardley had shown up in the Darklands so many months ago with an army of Spades behind him, Dinah had been amazed that the Spades had defected so easily from the Cards to join her side. Now that she had witnessed their living conditions, and the vein of unease that ran through the ranks, she understood completely. The Spades were desperate for change. It was her privilege as queen to be able to give it to them. Sir Gorrann, as usual, had been right about everything.

She let her weight shift from foot to foot, her thoughts lingering always on Alice or Wardley. The night huddled protectively around Dinah and her Yurkei guard. There was a faint creak of wood, the slightest of breezes, and the ominous feeling of darkness approaching. Dinah shut her eyes and willed herself to listen, as she held her breath in the pitch-black barracks. She could sense a man moving through the rooms like a cat on silent feet. He made no sound. Everything around her moved slowly, purposefully. A drop of water falling from the ceiling took years to reach the ground. A paper fluttered in the breeze, circling and dancing across the disgusting floor.

She felt Ki-ershan's mouth brush her ear.

"*Uhlaet.*" Breathe.

Another soft creak echoed through the room, and Dinah's spine tightened uncomfortably. She felt Ki-ershan's arm wrapped protectively around her, the beating of his furious Yurkei heart against her shoulder. She was not afraid, not for herself—no one would get through him.

From her hiding place, Dinah saw the rickety door swing open and watched as a tall shadow stepped into the room. Immediately, she recognized the black cloak and hood. It was the same terrifying ensemble that had come into her room that fateful night. The figure moved quickly. There was a flash of silver in the moonlight as he raised his dagger, creeping swiftly toward the slumbering lump on the bed. The figure looked quietly down at the sleeping Spade before yanking back the bedcovers, his dagger arching overhead.

He would not succeed. Sir Gorrann was ready and waiting for him. He threw the covers into the attacker's face, leaping from the bed and tackling the smaller man to the floor. With one hand, Sir Gorrann grabbed the cloaked man's dagger and tossed it across the room. Unleashing a growl, her loyal Spade crouched over the figure, his legs pinning down the man's arms, his long sword pressed tightly against his throat.

"Don't move, coward," he hissed. Sir Gorrann blew a lock of hair out of his face and nodded to the false wooden wall that Dinah and a dozen Spades stood behind, all too easy to miss with the new construction, riddled with holes perfect for spying. The wall dropped with a thud, and Dinah strode forward in a shower of black dust. Her steps were slow, calculated. Taking a deep breath, she steadied her face and withdrew her emotions. Now was not the time for feelings.

"Take off his hood."

Sir Gorrann pulled the man up to his knees and bound his hands behind him with rope. With a yank, he pulled off his hood. Cheshire's black hair shimmered in the light, a macabre grin twisting his narrow face.

"My queen, it is so nice to see you about at this late hour of night. What brings you here, beautiful daughter?"

Dinah smiled coldly before striking his cheek, hard, once and again. Cheshire barely winced. Her black eyes were emotionless as she stared into his face. "I know the truth. I know what you did. Confess it to me now, and you may have a prayer of going to your grave with a clear heart."

Cheshire's features hardened. He now looked incredibly dangerous, a coiled snake ready to strike. "What is it that you think you know, Your Grace?"

Dinah glowered down at him, rage building inside her at the sight of his snide smile. But she would not lose control like she had with Alice. *Never again*. Dinah seethed in his presence, the crown glittering brightly on her head.

"I know that you killed my brother. You killed Lucy and Quintrell that night, and then you threw—threw!—Charles from a window. You murdered him, a young child, the son of the woman you once loved. How could you? He was innocent!"

"He was a pawn!" hissed Cheshire. "He stood in the way of your throne by his very nature. He was a weakness, an embarrassment to you, to our family! He was the proof that your whore of a mother actually slept with the king. I knew the only way I could convince you that the king never intended to give you the crown was to get rid of Charles. It was the only way you would leave the palace, the only way you would ever *seize* your destiny. The king would have killed you if you had stayed. He would never have crowned you queen. I was only looking out for you. You must believe me."

"I do," said Dinah calmly. "But you were sloppy that night. So unlike you, Cheshire. You killed Charles, but you were in a hurry. You had to wake me and send me on my way, and also convince me that the king had killed him. Perfect timing was so crucial to your plan. In your haste, you took the crown that Charles made for me. *The only evidence of your crime.* You didn't anticipate that I would go to Charles's room before fleeing, that I would notice it was missing. But why would you anticipate that? That had to do with *love.* You would never, in your wildest manipulations, dream that I would go to my pathetic brother's room instead of fleeing for my life. But I did. You have never understood love."

Cheshire's eyes narrowed into glittering slits of black. "I believe you know a little about where love can lead a person, don't you? And you didn't love Charles. You pitied him. He was like a malignant growth—he needed to be cut off."

He gave her a cruel smile before chuckling. "Charles was silent, you know, when I threw him out the window. He curled up in my arms, like he had accepted his fate. There was no struggle. He had just watched me kill his beloved caretakers. What could he do? So the boy just let me drop him out the window. And as he fell to his death, he waved at me, right up until his body hit the stone. Why? Because he was mad—"

Dinah cut him off. "No. He waved at you because he knew I would discover the truth. Because he knew you would soon join him in that starless night that waits for all of us. He knew I would outsmart you eventually."

Dinah circled him now, sizing up his betrayal before gently resting her hand on his cheek, her fingers tracing the lines of his face. "Pride was your fatal mistake. You wanted to give me that crown, because of its glory, because of its grandness, and because you wanted Wonderland to *see it*. If you had kept it hidden forever, I would never have known. But you had to place it on my head and flaunt your genius, your stolen triumph. Your real reward was the moment when your daughter was crowned queen—the culmination of all your scheming."

Cheshire's smile stretched to the ends of his face, his dark eyes sparkling with pleasure, and he leaned in as if to rest his head on her shoulder. "Dinah, so fierce and intelligent, the pride of my loins. Tell me, how did you unravel my well-laid plans?"

Harris shuffled forward from behind the wall of Spades. His normally kind eyes filled with fury. "It was simple once Dinah spoke with Ruby Thorndike and Lord Geheim. After my queen fled the kingdom, you were nervous about having the crown on your person, especially with the king around. If he found out that you, and not the queen, had killed his son, nothing could have saved you from his anger. So you gave it to two men who owed you a debt—Lords Sander and Delmont—for safekeeping. Lord Sander agreed to keep the crown for you, in his home, for his debt was greater. Together, they began to put the pieces together and, in a fatal miscalculation, attempted to blackmail you. You poisoned Lord Delmont and his family as a warning to Lord Sander. An entire family, wiped out, all to scare one man. Your plan worked. Terrified, Lord Sander gave the crown to his apprentice, Swete Thorndike, to hide it from you. He thought it was his insurance—that you wouldn't kill him if you didn't know where the crown was."

Cheshire laughed, an insane, high-pitched cackle dripping with malice. "Those lords, so jumpy! They thought they could outsmart me. It makes me laugh even now."

Harris continued, "Then you left, to find Dinah, to help raise her army. You marched on the palace. You killed Lord Sander in the battle—how convenient to be able to do it out in the open!—and then, with a bribe, you were able to persuade a few Spades to kill his family." Harris paused for effect. "We have ferreted out those men, by the way. They will stand a private trial for murder."

"And then . . ." Cheshire's cool demeanor looked slightly worried now, his black eyes darting back and forth from Dinah's face to Sir Gorrann's.

Harris went on, "After you returned, you quickly figured out that Lord Sander had hidden the crown with his poor apprentice. One day before the queen's coronation, you snuck into the Thorndike residence, killed Swete, and found the crown he had been hiding. Then you gave it to Vittiore—Alice—to carry into the coronation." Harris rubbed his glasses. "You must have believed you were in the clear! To think, in your blind pride, you had forgotten what you had told the queen about your whereabouts the night of her brother's murder. That you had consorted with Lords Delmont and Sander while the king murdered her brother. I imagine their names must have been the easiest to remember in the midst of your lie, seeing how you had already killed one and were planning on killing the other. What a sloppy mistake! When the queen realized that Alice had never worn that crown, and that the King of Hearts had never even *seen* it, she realized it couldn't have been the king in the room that night. All this time it was you, the man in the shadows."

Cheshire smiled up at Dinah grimly, his face shaking with vicious intent. "So tell me, daughter, how does it feel to know that you started a war against a man who was innocent?"

Dinah didn't even blink.

"The King of Hearts wasn't innocent. He tried to kill me several times, though it's understandable, seeing how he believed that *I* actually killed Charles. Though our belief in the other one's guilt was false, I have no regrets. He was a terrible king, a murderer a thousand times over, and a corrupt leader. He threw those who opposed him in the Black Towers. He cheated and exploited the people of Wonderland. He ordered the slaughter of hundreds of Yurkei and those villagers who lived in the Twisted Wood."

Her eyes flitted briefly to Sir Gorrann.

"The king didn't protect his people when our armies took the palace. He took Alice from her home and attempted to use her to usurp my throne. Then he killed her mother right in front of her, as a warning to me. Trust me, I have no regrets about killing him."

Cheshire's eyes watched her face. "My little Dinah, so full of fury. But humor me one last time. How did you know that I would be here? A lucky guess?"

Cheshire's cracks were starting to show as his eyes darted wildly from face to face: Harris, flush with anger; Sir Gorrann, rippling with fury; and Dinah, cold and as still as stone.

She clicked her tongue and answered his question. "You are by far the most clever mind in Wonderland, and yet, like any man, you are still predictable. The calling card of Lord Cheshire is that he cleans up his messes. You make sure that anything in your way simply disappears. You and the king made sure that Faina Baker disappeared into the Black Towers, and that Alice disappeared completely into the creation of Vittiore. You killed not only Lords Delmont and

Sander, but also their families. You leave no trace behind, and you punish all those who were connected to your plans, even by the slightest margin. I'm going to guess that once you figured out that I was unraveling your plan—which was yesterday—you needed to get rid of those who would stand in your way when something happened to me.

"You came for Sir Gorrann first because he would be the most vocal and had the most power. I would guess Harris would be your next target, then Wardley."

"Wardley would rejoice at your death." Cheshire grinned. "His hatred for you will never fade."

Dinah's face stayed unaffected. Cheshire seemed to get aggravated by this and began squirming. His words rushed out in a screaming wave as his carefully constructed face fell to pieces.

"Don't just stand there, staring at me like that. I created you, Dinah! Without me, you would be no one. From the day you were born, a squalling, screaming child, I had a plan for you, a plan to raise you up to be queen. I protected you from the king's wrath. And oh, *how you were my child*. Your black hair, your intelligence, the way you watched people. But you also had your mother's delicate heart, prone to love. A flaw if I ever saw one. Every single day of my life, I worked so that you might be queen, so that my blood would become royal. I might have been born poor, but I would be the father to the queen someday. My plan unfolded the moment I saw your mother. I crept my way into her heart, so that someday we would create a child to rule. If I wasn't born into the Royal Line of Hearts, I would scheme my way into it. You have a crown on your head because I put it there. You marched on Wonderland Palace because I arranged it. And if you hadn't meddled where your nose didn't belong, we would have ruled the entire kingdom.

"In a few years' time, we would have marched on Hu-Yuhar and enslaved the Yurkei beneath us, something the King of Hearts only *dreamed* of. You would have been the most powerful ruler that Wonderland had ever known!"

His eyes were wild now as his voice rose through the barracks, hysterical. "Power, Dinah! True power! That's all that matters, and I've done everything to give it to you. If you wouldn't take it, then I would have." His eyes lingered on Dinah's face. "My plan was flawless."

Dinah reached down and rested her hand against Cheshire's wildly beating heart. "And yet, it was all ruined by a mad boy, who wanted nothing more than to give a gift to his sister. *Love* ruined your plans."

Cheshire stared into his daughter's face, his words cruel. "*Love* also ruined Wardley's life."

Dinah turned away. "Raise him to his feet."

Two Spades walked forward and propped him up. Sir Gorrann held his sword tightly against Cheshire's throat.

"You can't kill me. I'm your father!"

Dinah stepped forward, so close that he could feel her breath. Her face twisted in anger, her fingers clasped on both sides of his head. "Hear this!" she hissed quietly. "I have no father. Not you, and not the king. Too long have I been defined by the men who claimed that title. I had a loving mother, an innocent brother. And I have men who are truly loyal to me. I need no father."

Clearing her throat, she leaned back on her heels and regained her composure. She held out her arm over him, as if blessing him. "Cheshire of Verrader, I strip you of all lands and titles in your name."

Cheshire began to howl and writhe against the Spades that held him. "Dinah, no! I'm your father. I saved you. I helped you win a war. I gave you a crown!"

Dinah continued. "I disavow you from the council, and from the court. You are no longer a representative in our relations with the Yurkei. You have no power in any decision made for the good of Wonderland, now and forever. You are declared an enemy of Wonderland."

Cheshire's face distorted as it became racked with wretched sobs. "Please! Dinah, have mercy on me."

"You will have mercy, though not in the way you desire it. You deserve the Black Towers, to have your body and soul tortured for the rest of your days. You deserve the same fate to which you and the King of Hearts sent Faina Baker—a living hell!"

"You killed her daughter! You are not innocent like you believe." He let out a shriek of frustration.

Dinah closed her eyes for a moment. *He was right.* The truth of his words nestled in her heart. "Be thankful that I will not throw you in the Black Towers, for I do not trust the Black Towers to hold your deviousness, and they will not stand much longer. You are a poisonous snake in the grass, and if you are exiled, the day will come when I will find an army at my doorstep. You are the most dangerous creature in Wonderland."

Cheshire's legs lifted off the ground as he kicked and struggled. His deceitful words turned quickly into pleas. "Please, Dinah, for your mother. For your kingdom. We are family."

Dinah turned away from him, tying her cloak around her neck with a firm twist and pulling the hood over her crown. She turned and faced Cheshire again.

"Look now, and have your peace. Your daughter wears a crown, and will to the end of her days. Your grandchildren and those after them will bear the crown as well. Die knowing that your child will never again be manipulated or used, not by you or anyone else. Look upon my face. It is done. You killed my brother, and gods know how many other countless innocents who stood in your way over the years."

"Hundreds," hissed Cheshire. "Thousands."

Dinah bent and picked up Cheshire's dagger, the hilt inlaid with purple amethysts, the twin to her own. "I will keep this close to me always as a reminder of where I come from, and of the man that I never desire to be."

His face turned red now, full of anger. "You will never be rid of me. I have hundreds of people loyal to me, and they will not stop with my death. You will never be safe. Never!"

Now it was Dinah's turn to smile. "You have killed everyone who knew your secrets. There is no one left."

Cheshire's head dropped. He was defeated.

When he looked up again, a single tear trailed down his cheek. "Then I will rest in the knowledge that inside of you lies a part of me. A fury combined with a curious and deceptive mind, and every day you will wake with the yearning to release it."

Dinah turned away from him now, hiding her face from those around her as her mouth trembled. The room waited in silence. After a few moments, she inhaled and released a deep breath, letting her shoulders drop.

"Good-bye, Cheshire."

He began to scream as she walked toward the door, carefully avoiding the black roots that were twisting slightly nearer to her feet with each step. She paused at the opening and looked back. All she could see in the darkness now were his pointed white teeth, twisted up in a grin.

Sir Gorrann's voice rose over the clamor. "Orders, Your Majesty?"

Dinah paused, but only for a moment.

"Off with his head."

Eighteen

Weeks passed before Dinah felt Cheshire's haunting presence leave her. His body had been buried in the tunnels underneath the palace, his head taken to the Western Slope to be thrown into the sea. If there was anyone who could figure out how to come back from the dead, it would be Cheshire, and Dinah wasn't taking any chances.

The council had been reconfigured. There was no adviser to the queen, no head of the council. She would be influenced by no single person, rather by a multitude of wise men and, for the first time in history, wise women. *This was for the best.* Unlike the king before her, Dinah's decisions would be her own.

Dinah's mind wandered as she made her way to the new Spade barracks, Ki-ershan ever at her back. Things were moving quickly in Wonderland, and though Dinah dreamed of a time where she could hide in her room and cry over Cheshire's betrayal and the betrayal of her own heart, she couldn't. Not now. Not ever. She had taken Cheshire's head, and yet she was curiously free of guilt. She would miss his sharp mind, but every child in Wonderland was safer without his convincing tongue twisting lies in her ear. Of this she was certain.

The new Spade barracks were being built on the western side of the palace, though they would be much smaller than the first ones. Now that the Spades could marry, they would need less housing, as most would take wives and houses in Wonderland proper. Sir Gorrann happily oversaw the construction, and under his rule, the Spades were beginning to show a bit of pride and decorum. They were still a disgusting and vile group, but the changes were evident—no Spade had killed another in weeks. This was a very encouraging sign.

Dinah found Sir Gorrann perched on a stump among towering piles of white logs. One hand held a hammer, the other a
cherry tart. He stood and bowed awkwardly.

"My queen."

She sat down beside him. "How are things progressing?"

He turned to survey the construction. The new barracks were to be white, inlaid with black stones carved into
the Spade symbol. They would be very similar to the barracks for the Heart Cards.

"Slowly, as always, but it looks to be quite a good place
for a man to spend the rest of his days."

Dinah rested her hand against his shoulder. "Tell me,
Sir Gorrann, have you reconsidered marrying again? I hear
that the girls in Wonderland proper can barely keep up with
proposals from the Spades."

He smiled grimly. "No. As yeh know, there is only Amabel. She will be the keeper of my heart until my last breath."

"Which I hope won't be soon. We have much to do."

He let out a groan. "So yeh keep reminding me. I will
barely finish these barracks before yeh have me starting on
the new prison. Yer a slave driver, yeh are! Emptying the

Black Towers is going to be a massive task. It's going to take us years, yeh know."

"So I've heard. Nonetheless, we must start soon." *The Black Towers.* Dinah rubbed her forehead. She had quickly passed a new law that forbade strapping prisoners against the walls of the towers, but there was still so much legislating to be done. The Clubs had aggressively pressed back against building a new prison system, but relented when Dinah involved them in the planning and construction of the building.

The Spades would aid in the plans and building as well. She hoped that the activity would bond the two groups. *We'll see*, she thought. Dinah had learned quickly that each faction of the Cards had a distinct voice, and the best way to acknowledge those voices was to listen honestly. Ruling had a learning curve, and she hoped that in ten years it would be easier.

Dinah bowed her head in Sir Gorrann's direction. "Please thank the Spades for all their work. I will send some refreshments their way this evening from the kitchens. And thank you."

Sir Gorrann's gold eyes met hers. Lately, there was a renewed energy in them. "Thank yeh, my queen. Will I see yeh for sparring this week?"

"Yes. Four o'clock, tomorrow. Don't be late again. Harris swings his pocket watch so violently when schedules are ignored, it's likely to cut off our heads one of these times."

Dinah gave a shallow laugh, suddenly reminded of Cheshire . . . and Alice. She grew silent. Sir Gorrann saw her withdraw and rested his hand gently against Dinah's head. "When I look at yeh, I don't see Cheshire. Yeh are yer own person, Dinah. And, with work, yeh will be a great queen."

Dinah blushed.

"Are you finally headed there tonight? To see *him*?"

She nodded. "I think it's time."

His eyes met hers, and Dinah saw a sympathetic look pass through them.

"Very good, Dinah. Though it will be torture for yeh, it is the right decision for yer kingdom."

"Good day, Sir Gorrann."

"Good day, Yer Majesty," he said before returning to his tart.

She sighed and headed back to the palace. There were councils, meetings, and a banquet to attend later. A visit to the Hearts, to the Clubs, to the court. Dinah's life was not her own, and yet she couldn't be more thankful, for those things meant a kingdom. But first, there was one last terrible thing.

The time had come to ask. It was late afternoon, the prettiest part of the day. The blazing jewel of a sun cast a pink shadow over all of Wonderland just as it began to set.

Dinah pulled a simple black-and-white dress over her head and settled the lighter ruby crown upon her brow. Two bejeweled heart pins swept her hair up in a small bun. While she loved Charles's crown, it was terribly heavy, and she only wore it when she had official business to attend to or when she would be seen by large crowds. Tonight featured neither of those activities.

Ki-ershan's scowling blue eyes glimmered in the mirror's reflection. He was upset with her. She turned.

"I must go alone. Please understand. It's just a quick jaunt through the palace. I'll be safe."

Ki-ershan turned away from her, his muscular arms

folded in protest. *A pouting Yurkei*, she thought, *is something I never thought I would see in my lifetime.*

"I'm sorry. I'll be back. You understand why you can't come."

"I'll follow you from a respectable distance and stand outside the room."

"If you must."

"I must, Queen of Hearts."

♥

Dinah slipped out of the door and made her way quickly through the palace to the Royal Apartments. She couldn't hear him behind her, even if she knew he was there.

She dreaded visiting this side of the palace. Charles's and Alice's rooms were located here, and both haunted Dinah's mind with dark memories. Alice's room was now occupied by Wardley, who had become a recluse in every way. When she reached the door, Dinah took a deep breath, steeling her heart against the words she knew would rip her soul to shreds. Of all the things she had done—joining the Yurkei and the Spades together, marching on the palace, choosing to free herself from Cheshire's influence—she knew that the future of her kingdom depended most on what happened in the next few minutes.

Dinah exhaled, knocked once, and entered. Alice's once whimsical bedchambers, breezy and lovely, had been destroyed. Dresses and linens were shredded and hung from the rafters. Paintings had been slashed, furniture overturned, and food and refuse left to rot. A stench hit her nostrils: human sweat, waste, and agony. Gryphon, the white peacock who had tried to protect his mistress, strolled proudly over the mess, seemingly oblivious to the hole in which he lived. He pecked at crumbs on the floor.

Light from the setting sun flickered over Dinah's face as she looked toward Wardley, who stood precariously on the windowsill. Dinah's heart clutched—a fall would lead to certain death in the hedge gardens below. Still, she didn't flinch. She was told that he did this often, sometimes even letting his foot dangle off the edge. But he never jumped. Hopefully, her presence didn't inspire the leap. She walked toward him with small, careful steps.

"Do you think I could fly?" he asked. "To where she is?"

Dinah made no sound. He didn't turn around to look at her face.

Finally, after several moments of silence, Wardley sighed. "What do you want, Dinah?"

His voice broke her heart. It was bare, stripped of every passion that had once lilted and raised its cadence. The anger had departed from him, and there was only grief left. Wardley was a hollow shell of the man he once was. She had cut out his heart, just as Iu-Hora had warned.

"I'll ask once more. What do you want?"

"I think you know," she replied softly.

"I heard you had Cheshire killed. One more body to add to your growing count. Two dead fathers. It must feel wonderful to have so much power."

"There will be no more," she replied plainly. "There can't be. The rage of the Queen of Hearts must end."

"Why does that concern me?"

He looked over his shoulder at her. His hair was longer, his eyes hollow and sunken. It pained Dinah to see him like this. She had never dreamed that seeing this devastation on his face would hurt more than seeing him entwined with Alice. This was part of her penance, forcing herself to look upon his face every day. This alone would humble and break her. It was something she wanted, something she needed. The all-consuming and hungry fury lived inside her, and it would need drowning daily. Wardley now stared at her, clenching his jaw as he struggled to control his emotions.

"Please go, Dinah. I can't bear to look at you." He blinked slowly, as if keeping his eyes open took what little strength he had left. Dinah walked slowly toward him, her hand outstretched. He did not reach for her in return, but rather watched with curious eyes. Once Dinah reached the window, she knelt before him.

"What are you doing?" Wardley stared down, unnerved by her behavior. "This is ridiculous. You're the queen. Get up."

"Be my king," she said plainly. "Be my king, Wardley Ghane."

"You can't be serious."

"Be my king," she replied, her knees pressed against a clod of dirt. "My kingdom deserves a righteous ruler. I cannot be that ruler alone. I fear my own nature, and I need someone to temper it. A fair king. A *good* king. Someone patient, wise, and kind, someone who is good at his very core. Someone who will make the right decisions for the kingdom again and again, someone who can steady his anger, and stay his hand. I can be the face and strength of Wonderland, but I need someone to be its heart. And it can only be you."

She raised her head to look at his face. "You are the heart that this kingdom deserves."

A tear dripped down Wardley's cheek. It landed near Dinah's outstretched hand.

"You killed her. You killed Alice!" He shook his head. "I cannot forgive you."

Dinah closed her eyes against the hot flood of tears that threatened to spill out over the floor. "I don't need you to forgive me. I need you to be my king. I need your steady hands on this kingdom, along with mine." Dinah crawled up to his feet, her head still bowed. "Together, we can change everything, for the better. Don't say yes for me. Say yes for every man, woman, and child out there. Say yes for Faina Baker, and for Bah-kan, for Emily, for Swete Thorndike, for every person who will die if I turn out like either of my fathers. Say yes for Alice, and know that she will forever haunt my dreams and waking hours."

She raised her head up so that her black eyes met Wardley's red-rimmed ones. "I'm so sorry, Wardley. For everything. You must believe me."

He blinked twice and clenched his fists. "I believe that you are sorry, *right this moment*. But I also believe that once your rage rises inside of you, you would lose control again. You have a darkness that you can't control. But you also have the potential to be a great queen. How infuriating it is that somehow I still believe that, even with all you have done. I almost died a thousand times for your right to be queen, because I believed in you. I have seen your heart in all its radiant goodness. It is there, buried beneath the layers left by your fathers. But I can't love you. How can I be your king when being near you makes me long to wrap my hands around your neck? How can I be your husband?"

"Not without difficulty," responded Dinah, her eyes cast to the ground. "But it would be what is best for Wonderland. It is your fate to become the next King of Hearts."

Wardley let out a long exhale as he turned back to the

window. "I will think on it. That is all I can promise. Know that things will never change between us. I will not grow to love you as you desire, nor do I believe that I could ever be your friend again." His voice choked. "Not for Alice. My love, my dead love."

A sob overtook him.

Dinah turned to leave, her heart breaking. Her jeweled slipper hesitated near the threshold. "Wardley, one thing: if you become king, you can't tell anyone. You can't tell anyone what happened to Alice. If Mundoo ever found out . . ."

"I won't," sniffed Wardley. "She disappeared into the night. Cheshire made sure of that."

Dinah reached for the latch on the door.

"Wait."

She paused and turned back, her heart hopeful. Wardley looked at her, his face alarmed. "I told someone."

Dinah's heart began to hammer. "What? Who did you tell?"

Wardley sighed and rubbed his face. "That night that I met with you, outside by the Julla Tree, I was distraught. Alice was gone, and I was filled with vile, murderous thoughts. I dreamed of killing you. I had to escape. After the Cards out-side my door fell asleep, I climbed out of my window and made my way down through the kitchens. I ran until I col-lapsed with exhaustion. I began to lose consciousness. I had brought my dagger with me. I wanted to die, Dinah. You did that to me."

Dinah closed her eyes, heavy guilt falling around her.

"I tried to cut my throat, but my arms kept shaking, and so instead I fell asleep with the dagger clutched against my chest. Sleep took me so quickly; I hadn't slept in days. When I woke up there was a man—a traveler—standing over me."

Wardley shook his head and sat down on the window-sill, his long legs dangling over the edge. "The man's name was Lewis. I've never met a man like him before. He *knew* things. He had a way with words, a lyrical tongue, and a sharp mind. He invited me back to his tent, but by which way I cannot fathom; this man had somehow salvaged a pot of Iu-Hora's blue smoke.

"He opened it, and the tent filled with smoke. Dinah, I told the man *everything*. Everything about you, Cheshire,

Alice, the Cards, Iu-Hora, the battle. And when I awoke, he was gone."

Dinah tilted her head. "Why did you come back at all?"

He turned to the window. "I can't say. Maybe I have to believe that there are still wonders out there for me, even if she is gone."

Dinah turned the handle on the door and brushed her hot tears away. "Thank you for telling me. Consider what I said, please."

Wardley nodded, his eyes looking toward the Western Slope. "You weren't painted very well in the story. A villain for the ages."

Dinah stared back at his figure illuminated on the windowsill, the wind blowing his hair in tiny circles.

"I deserve it." She shut the door behind her.

The traveler proved impossible to find, and though Dinah used every resource available, it was as if he had fallen down a rabbit hole.

Nineteen

The seasons of the court began in full swing as Dinah waited for Wardley to make his decision. It was an exhausting stretch of balls, banquets, meetings, and pointless introductions to people that Dinah knew she would never speak with again.

Just that evening Dinah had hosted a banquet welcoming the new ladies and lords of the court. The Queen of Hearts made her usual endless rounds of pleasantries and small talk, laughing too loudly at jokes that she didn't find funny, nodding at gentlemen who worked too hard to catch her eye. Royal life was exhausting, but she reminded herself that a good queen understood the dictates of social politics. This was her duty, her privilege. It was tiresome, but as Harris kept reminding her, not optional.

Still, her mind was only on Wardley, and when she returned to her room with sore feet and ribs, Dinah hoped to find an envelope waiting for her with his answer. There was no envelope, but this time there was something: a small carving left outside her door. Dinah smiled as she picked it up, turning it in the light. It was a wooden sea horse. She remembered the day she had given an identical one to Charles.

It wasn't a yes. But it wasn't a no either.

She stepped inside her chambers, and with a happy sigh, she made quick work of stripping off her gown with relish. Finally unburdened of the weight of the rose-scented fabric, she stepped out onto the balcony in the cool night air, wearing only a thin gray nightgown that swirled around her thighs. So much had changed, yet her view remained the same; all of Wonderland proper and the endless fields of wildflowers in the North were now turning a pinkish red. To the east, she could vaguely make out the dormant, topless

Yurkei Mountains just past the Twisted Wood. *Her kingdom*, which had come at the greatest cost.

A bitter wind danced around her, and she heard the low moans of the trees in the Twisted Wood carry over the land, a sound she no longer found terrifying. To her, the sound was comforting, like the trees were calling her back to their mysteries. Her hair blew around her face as she caught the hint of a black shadow moving swiftly over the ground. Dinah squinted. *It couldn't be.* She ran to the edge of the balcony. *It was.*

She flew toward the door, yelling to Ki-ershan as she ran from her chambers. Soon she was sprinting through the palace, Ki-ershan loping behind her, peppering her with questions she fully ignored. A black cat, so dark he was almost plum, gave a lazy yawn as she raced past, licking his paws with contentment. Faster her feet flew through the hallways, then the courtyards, past the stables and toward the devastated iron gates. Three Spades stood guard, rushing to open the gates for their beloved queen while confused looks passed silently between them.

"Hurry!" she shouted. "Please! Open the gates! Faster!"

With a clang, the gates slowly opened, only wide enough for Dinah to slip through. She felt the cool grass beneath her feet, and the faintest bite of autumn nipping at her ankles. When she reached the cusp of the hill that overlooked the palace, she stopped running. She bent over to catch her breath, getting dizzy. Ki-ershan stayed back, hesitant for the first time since he had become her guard. There was a danger here not even he could overcome. Dinah reached out her trembling hand.

Morte was badly hurt. Jagged scars ran the length of his body, and some traces of white Yurkei paint still lingered from battle. He was missing a large chunk of flesh beneath his left ear, where his blood had dried into a thick crust. Bone spikes on both of his back hooves were broken or dangling from their stumps, the raw marrow exposed. An arrow was buried deep in his flank, and each time he took a step, blood and greenish fluid seeped from the infected wound.

Morte stepped back with caution when Dinah approached him, letting out a nervous whinny as she reached toward his nose. As her fingertips brushed his nostril, he bucked backward. Dinah ducked as one of his bone spurs almost took her eye. His teeth snapped at her hand.

"Shhh . . . shhh . . ."

"Your Majesty?" Ki-ershan hissed. "He is probably wild with infection."

"He'll be fine." Dinah repeated it again and again, until she too was convinced.

Letting out a deep breath, she bowed her head low before him. Then she reached out and gingerly placed her hand on Morte's side, running it up and over his wounds. She walked around him with timid steps, taking in each injury.

Morte seemed unsure of who she was. When her hand returned to his nose, he jerked away, his hooves plowing long furrows in the earth. She walked in front of him and raised her head to stare into his huge black eyes. Again, Dinah lifted her hand to his muzzle, where he eventually bent to smell it. The smell of war still drifted from his mane as it blew around them. Together they stood silently as the sky around them lit up with moving stars, each one leaving a bright streak as it traveled toward the sea.

With reluctance, Morte finally let out a hiss of steam from his torn nostril, bent his head, and lifted his hoof. Dinah stepped carefully on it, her bare feet screaming in pain as the bone spikes pressed into her flesh. Using his mane, she pulled herself snugly across his neck, her legs falling so easily into the grooves of his shoulders. His back, that black ocean of hard muscle, welcomed her home, and she nuzzled down against him, feeling his gigantic ribs contract and expand.

From atop his back, she could see the dazzling spires of Wonderland Palace and the red glow that the palace cast on the land around it. From here she could imagine the small lives taking place; Harris, asleep in the library, glasses sliding off the end of his nose; Sir Gorrann, tossing back some ale as he chuckled among fellow Spades; and Wardley, staring out across the land with a burdened heart, wondering how much he would give for his kingdom.

Her absent crown weighed heavy against her head as she clicked her tongue and gave the slightest of kicks against Morte's sides.

"Let's go home," she whispered.

After a moment of hesitation, Morte began an unsteady walk toward the palace, step after tender step. Dinah clutched his black hair and leaned her head against his thick neck. Her heart sang that he had returned to her, and that this broken thing was not beyond saving. Together they made their way back to the palace that had once been a prison for them both. As he walked, Dinah felt the beat of his heart thundering up from his chest, its chaotic lullaby so angry and yet so strong. A heart that beat much like her own.

EPILOGUE

Fifteen Years Later

The place was different than Dinah remembered it. The overgrown weeds were shorter, the foliage was not as heavy. The heads were still there, as stunning as the first time she had seen them. Their unsmiling mouths sat frozen as tall white ferns brushed up against them, tickling the faces of giants. The bright grass that Dinah remembered so vividly remained there; it was still a glowing, unearthly green.

The heads were still massive, and Dinah was glad to see that fear had not twisted her memory to remember things as grander than they actually were. Their etched gazes still seemed to pierce right through her chest. Some of the heads lay on their sides, others were completely upside down. She pointed. "There he is."

Dinah urged Morte closer from where they perched at the top of the hill. She turned her face sideways to look at one particular face and crown.

"It's him."

The bronze head of the deceased King of Hearts rested upside down on the ground, propped on his crown, with his mouth open in an angry scream. Some happy breed of mottled purple birds had made a nest in his mouth, and she watched with curiosity as they fluttered in and out between his teeth. At first glance, his wide eyes reminded her of Charles, but only for a second.

She smiled and reached down to unhook a clutch of wildflowers that rested on her saddle. She climbed off Morte and landed with a hard grunt. Getting on and off was just a little bit harder now. She had grown a bit less graceful with age, though many said the handsome queen had never been stronger. She knelt down next to the statue and arranged the lavender flowers so they draped gracefully across the tip of his crown.

Dinah glanced back at Wardley. "I think I'm going to look around a bit."

He nodded at her. "Stay by the heads. There are wild animals in this wood."

She knew it well.

The King of Hearts gave her the smallest of smiles, though sometimes it seemed to hurt his face to do so. Dinah would take it. Wardley was mostly quiet in her presence, but strong and firm when with others. His tender brown eyes had recently taken on a peaceful gaze underneath the crown her father once wore. As she walked away, she could feel the curious gaze of her husband piercing her chest. She turned back to look at him, but he was staring at the sky, something he did often.

Dinah turned and wandered through the Twisted Wood, taking in each head. Her empathy for them was much deeper than it had been last time. Ruling was not for the faint of spirit, and she could no more judge those who'd held the crown before her than she could her own heart.

The heads of the Yurkei chiefs were here as well, situated together in a tight cluster at the end of the valley. The strong heads of handsome warriors were crowned not with a piece of gold or silver, but with feathers or elaborate fabric swirls that trailed down over their faces. The eyes of the Yurkei made her feel as if they were watching her as she walked along, touching each face, marveling at its size and beauty. She found Mundoo's head standing upright, a cascade of feathers down the side of his temple. His eyes were made out of blue sapphires that glimmered and danced in the canopied sunlight. Fitting for the hero of his people, and a dear friend.

She tucked a second bunch of flowers across his feathered head and smiled at the uncanny likeness. Mundoo had been in fierce form when she saw him a week ago, when they had met to exchange Morte's newest offspring. The peace treaty held, and her yearly trips to Hu-Yuhar had become a beloved tradition of both Wonderlanders and the Yurkei. Now, the celebration of the newest Hornhoov colt eclipsed even the Royal Croquet Game. She smiled. Then again, what wouldn't Wonderlanders use as an excuse for a lavish party?

She walked past the statues, her boots crunching in the wet twigs. *Who made these, and why?* She would never know.

Not a fearful child any longer, she found the valley strangely beautiful—a perfect place for kings and queens to find their royal rest both during their life and after death.

Beyond a thick gathering of white trees, a clearing caught her eye. She pushed through a curtain of white moss, feeling her breath catch in her throat. The grass here was green and short, not unlike the grass on the croquet grounds at home. The ground in this clearing was covered with pale blue flowers, the morning dew glistening on their flat petals. *There she was.*

Dinah's gray stone head sat straight and tall, with Charles's crown upon her head. Her sculpted short black hair fell like a waterfall on the sides of her face. No jewels sat around her neck. Her eyes were carved from black obsidian, narrowed in fury. Her mouth curved up in a half smile, and though her eyes were angry, her face was serene, carved forever with a look of wisdom. The crown was perfect in its replication. Dinah absently ran her fingers over the sharp

tips upon her actual head. She stared at her likeness in wonder, thinking that this was a very strange feeling indeed.

From high above, the trees let out a deep groan. Dinah
watched as the woods rippled like water. Several trunks
twisted in her direction. Something rumbled in the foliage next to her, and Dinah's hand went to her sword. She
heard high shrieks and what sounded like a thousand tiny
feet crashing over ancient roots, destroying the sacred peace
of the Twisted Wood. A smile crept over her face as three
now-filthy children exploded out from the bushes and circled around her.

"Mama, did you see it? Did you see? It's you!"

Dinah scooped up Davi, her youngest daughter, as
Amabel and Charles, her nine-year-old twins, tugged at
each other and pointed. They ran around the head several
times before they tumbled to the ground, shrieking with
laughter. They wrestled like puppies around Morte, shoving
each other as he looked at them with annoyance. Finally,
they came to a stop at Dinah's feet.

"That's you!" Charles, the spitting image of his father,
said. He put his hands on his hips and his ruddy cheeks

flushed. "I want my own head when I'm king."

Dinah rested her hand on his cheek. "You'll have one, love. Someday you and Amabel will both rest here in the Valley of Heads."

Charles turned to his twin sister. "I bet when your head is here, it'll be covered with crane droppings!"

Amabel shoved him hard, and before Dinah could intervene they were running, a swirl of dirt and insults mixed with sibling familiarity like a cloud around them. Wardley descended on them, and soon he was hauling them apart.

"You two! Is this the way that princes and princesses should act?" he asked, trying to keep the smile off his face.

They both looked at the ground.

"Now, forgive each other so we can go look at the rest of the heads."

Amabel reluctantly hugged her brother before Wardley lifted her up and kissed her hard on both cheeks, a fierce love for his children dancing over his face. The King of Hearts didn't smile often, but it was always his children that made his face transform into the Wardley Dinah remembered, the carefree boy with flour dashed across his mouth. He lived for his children, and they adored him.

"We should go now," Wardley intoned to Ki-ershan, who sat nearby on a gray-speckled Hornhoov. Ki-ershan nodded silently. Charles hung on Wardley's right hand and Amabel on his left as the King of Hearts dragged the giggling twins after him, disappearing behind the white moss curtain.

Dinah turned back to her youngest daughter, so still and silent, always watching. Of all the children, six-year-old Davi looked the most like her—hair black as a raven's wing, eyes such a dark brown that they glittered like ink. Davi was lean and long, and much more clever than her two older siblings. She was sensitive and easily hurt, a quality Dinah loved. At times, she could be quietly thoughtful and kind to her family. Those days, when Dinah looked at her, she saw the best parts of herself. There were other times, though, when she was bullied by her older siblings and stared at them with such a consuming envy that it alarmed Wardley. After that, Davi would retreat into her own isolated world. Dinah stayed silent, because she could see that her daughter wasn't removing herself for anyone else's sake; Davi was plotting. On those days, when Dinah looked at her daughter, she saw someone else.

With a soft smile, Dinah curled her arms around her. "What's the matter?" Dinah nodded to the statue of her head. "Does it scare you?"

Davi nodded and buried her head against Dinah's shoulder. "I don't like it."

Dinah ran her hand over Davi's dark hair. "It's just a stone. It's not me."

"Does it mean you will die?"

"Someday. But not soon."

Davi whimpered. "I don't want you to leave. I wish you could stay forever."

Dinah pressed her red lips against Davi's cool cheeks. "Would that I could, my darling."

Morte trotted up beside them, and with a smile, Dinah put her tiny daughter on his still back. Davi shrieked with laughter.

"Look how high I am!"

Davi's face grew determined, her eyes glinting in a way that caused Dinah's heart to twist uncomfortably.

"Look, Mama! I am higher than Amabel *and* Charles!" She reached her hand down to Dinah's head. "Can I hold it? Please, Mama?"

It was the question she asked every day.

With a grimace, Dinah removed the heavy crown from her head and handed it to Davi, who placed it on her small head. It slipped over her eyes and she laughed. Then Davi stood on Morte's back and pointed at the sky.

"Look at me, Mama! I am the queen!" Her black eyes glittered in the filtered light of the Twisted Wood. "I am the queen!"

When she looked at her daughter's face, Dinah could feel the love for her child snaking its way around the black fury inside her. The fury would always remain, alive and hungry. But for her daughter's sake, Dinah prayed that this time, love would be enough to quench the flame.

"Begin at the beginning," the King said gravely, *"and go on till you come to the end: then stop."*

—Alice's Adventures in Wonderland *by Lewis Carroll*

ACKNOWLEDGMENTS

First and foremost, thank you to those who have stuck with Dinah until the very end of the series. Queen of Hearts was unique in that it had two lives—two births, two second novels, and then one bloody ending. If you were one of the first readers of the series, thank you for waiting a very long time for the last book. If you were a new reader, thank you for taking a chance on a very different sort of read. I hope that Dinah broke your heart and restored it.

I'm happy to get to thank those who have personally stood by me as the queen takes her final bow. Being surrounded by encouragement made it easy to pursue this career and this story.

Thank you to Emilia Rhodes and the team at HarperCollins

for all their dedication in getting Dinah into the hands of so many YA readers. Emilia, thank you for believing in this story and not insisting I change the ending. You understand Dinah so well, and by extension, myself as well. Taking Queen on was a risk, and it is a reflection of your brave nature that you believed in this story enough to give it a second life. Thank you also to the talented Alice Jerman and the editors at HarperCollins who have helped me plow through three novels now. A special thanks must go out to Gina Rizzo and Elizabeth Ward at Harper for crafting such a unique PR story for Queen. All the love in the world goes out to Jenna Stempel, who has designed the most beautiful covers that I've ever seen. Every time I see the Queen of Hearts covers, I marvel at how they are truly works of art.

Thank you to my agent, Jen Unter, who has helped the Queen of Hearts series along in a million small ways and is always encouraging. I'm glad I had you fighting for this. Thank you to Crystal Patriarche and the entire marvelous team at SparkPress in Arizona who have supported this book from the *very* beginning. You guys believed in Queen before there was a Queen.

To my writing partners and dear friends Emily Kiebel, Brianna Shrum, and Mason Torall, thanks for your weird brilliance. Each of you has a creepy Cheshire-like hand meddling in my work in the best of ways.

To my superb group of friends who have never stopped encouraging me and never complain about attending so many damn book signings: Nicole London, who inspires me to live creatively; Elizabeth Wagner, whose mind is a magical, hysterical place; Katie Hall, who fights so much for those she loves; Kim Stein, the sister of my heart and soul; Karen Groves, who turns my fury into mercy and my tears into laughter; Erin Chan, whose art rises above; Cassandra Splittgerber, who reminds me what is important; Katie Blumhorst, who is the best kind of sister-in-law; Emily Kiebel, who listened to me rattle off this plot in a manic pizza session; and to Amanda Sanders and Erin Burt, coven ladies who make me believe I can do anything.

To my beta readers who took the first crack at Queen, who loved fierce Dinah for the way she was: Erika, Michelle, Jeni, Jen, Patty, Sarah, Angela, Holly, Erin, and Stephanie—thank you for your words of advice and your belief in the story.

Finally, to my family, who continues to astonish me daily with the love they give. To Ryan Oakes, there aren't enough words to thank you. You believe in me, you encourage me, you stood for me when others doubted this story. You always have my back. I love you. Wardley's good heart is your own. To Maine—this dark heart broke wide open for you. Thank god it will never be the same. For Cindy, I love you. Best sister ever. Sorry you have to hang out with authors all the time now. To my parents, Ron and Tricia McCulley, who believed my fourth-grade teacher when she said they had a writer on their hands. To Denise McCulley and Butch and Lynette Oakes, I'm so glad I get to be part of your family.

To readers: may your broken hearts beat strong.

Have you read them all?

ONLY QUEENS WITH HEARTS CAN BLEED

HarperCollins *Children's Books*

BOOKS BY COLLEEN OAKES

Queen of Hearts

Blood of Wonderland

War of the Cards